i-ssassins

CHRISTOPHER EDGE

www.pearsonschoolsandfecolleges.co.uk

✓ Free online support
✓ Useful weblinks
✓ 24 hour online ordering

0845 630 33 33

Heinemann

Part of Pearson

Heinemann is an imprint of Pearson Education Limited, Edinburgh Gate, Harlow, Essex, CM20 2JE.

www.pearsonschoolsandfecolleges.co.uk

Heinemann is a registered trademark of Pearson Education Limited

Text © Christopher Edge 2011
Typeset by Kamae Design
Cover design by Craft Design
Cover images © Pearson Education Ltd/Jules Selmes (Building) and AYAKOVLEV.COM/
Shutterstock (Dancer)

The rights of Christopher Edge to be identified as author of this work have been
asserted by him in accordance with the Copyright, Designs and Patents Act 1988.

First published 2011

15 14 13
10 9 8 7 6 5 4 3

British Library Cataloguing in Publication Data
A catalogue record for this book is available from the British Library

ISBN 978 0 435 04601 9

Printed in China (EPC/03)

To find out more about Christopher Edge and his books, visit
www.christopheredge.co.uk

For Alex,
an adventure

CONTENTS

Non-fiction:

PROLOGUE

You never forget your first kill.

That's what they told me when I joined the Elite. Nothing compares to the sweet rush of adrenalin you get when you wipe somebody out of existence forever.

You forget all the hard work, the hours spent hunched in front of a screen stalking your prey, hunting them down. The long days tracing every step that they take, shadowing their every action. And when you make the final move to end it all, time seems to slow to a crawl as you watch their life drain away in a blizzard of zeroes and ones.

Don't worry, I'm not talking about a knife in the back or a bullet to the head. When I make a kill, there's no blood on the floor. It's all much cleaner than that. I can erase someone completely and they won't even feel a thing.

Confused? Let me explain. Think about what you really need to live. The money in your bank account, the contacts in your phone, the life-support system you plug into every time you go online.

Now think about the footprints you leave behind. The fragments of data floating in cyberspace: status updates, blog posts, tweets. Every search that you make, everything that you buy. Every byte of information that tells you who you are. Birth certificates, medical records, credit checks. I can see it all and I can take it all away with a single click of the mouse.

Profiles deleted, bank accounts purged, records wiped. Everything that you need to live in the twenty-first century gone in a split second. That's what it means to go in for the kill.

We're the ghosts in the machine. Cyberspace assassins. This country's last line of defence against the invisible enemies that plague us. The Elite.

The ultimate job – the ultimate thrill. With a computer at my fingertips, I'm invincible. Bulletproof. Nobody can touch me.

So how did I end up here – my hands scrabbling for a grip on a slippery steel cable as the lift cage below speeds towards me? I glance across at the filthy red numbers stamped inside the lift shaft. Floor 53. Forty-seven to go. Blood drips though my fingers as the cable cuts into my skin.

Inside that cage are two men armed with AK-47s who are hunting me down. As I climb this skyscraper in the heart of London's Canary Wharf, every single person inside the building wants me dead. Security guards, office workers, cleaning staff – they would all kill me without a second thought.

My hand slips and, for a heart-wrenching moment, my legs kick against empty air. I can hear the harsh grinding of lift gears as the cage comes towards me. If I fall now, it's all over.

With my hand flailing against the void, I reach up in desperation. The lift shaft fills with a screeching howl – the deafening sound the last thing I hear. Then my blood-slicked fingertips grab hold of the concrete sill.

As the last reserves of strength ebb from my body, I fling my other arm up, fingers clawing against concrete, and then haul my shaking body into the narrow recess between the lift shaft and the concrete wall. I lie there, my face pressed against the cold stone sill. Breath judders from my body in shuddering gasps.

I've never felt so alive.

The skyscraper shakes with a hideous whine as the lift cage approaches. Grinding gears pass centimetres from my face. Then the muffled sound of the men's voices echo from the cage as it climbs above me.

I'll tell you how I got here – about everything that happened to me from the first moment I heard about the Elite. I just need to make sure I stay alive long enough to finish the story.

CHAPTER ONE

From the window of my apartment, I could see London spread out before me. Its skyscrapers and gleaming offices. The gothic spires of the Houses of Parliament and the glittering spokes of the Millennium Wheel. All following the curve of the River Thames.

A two-million-pound view, that's what the estate agent who sold the penthouse said to me. *Are you sure your parents can afford it?* I transferred the money into the estate agency's bank account later that day. Behind me, a 62-inch 3D TV hung from one wall of the apartment, blaring out the football match from surround-sound speakers. Littered around the place were pieces of the latest hi-tech kit: games consoles, mixing decks, smartphones and laptops. Every gadget that money could buy.

My name's Luke Kitson. I'm fourteen years old and I live here alone. No parents. No school. No worries.

Do you want to know how I did it? I can't tell you everything – I've got to keep a few trade secrets, but I'll let you know one thing. All I needed was a computer.

In the far distance, an ugly tower block squatted on the skyline. A grim reminder of where I came from. You see, I didn't always live like this. My name used to be Harrison

Andrews. I lived with my gran in a poky two-bedroom flat on a run-down estate, just north of the Watford Gap. The only thing she ever told me about my parents was that they didn't want me. That was fine – I didn't want them either. But I wanted out.

At school, most people thought I was some kind of geek because I spent all my free time holed up in the computer suite. I didn't care – most of my friends were online anyway. While they played video games, I was searching the Internet for ways to escape. That's when I came up with my plan.

I'd always been smart when it came to computers – knowing how to get them to do what I wanted them to do. At first I just played around on the school's computer network. Most of my teachers were too lazy to bother to change their passwords regularly, so it was easy to crack into the system. Once inside, I could change my grades, improve my attendance record, even find out the questions for next week's Maths test – all with just a click of the mouse. That's when I realised how profitable my computer skills could be. But when every single person in my class scored a hundred per cent in a Maths test, I learned the importance of covering my tracks.

After that, I graduated to sharpening my skills in the wilds of the World Wide Web. Everything I wanted to know was out there. With a bit of practice, I was soon able to sneak past the security systems of most websites, creeping through the back doors left behind by the coders who built them. Cracking passwords, dodging firewalls, accessing encrypted files. Whatever I wanted, if it was on the Internet, then I could find a way inside. Some people might call it hacking, but I preferred to call myself a digital explorer.

As I explored, I discovered a whole new world – one that I realised could give me a brand-new life. But then, when I popped back home for lunch on the last day of the school term, the real world broke back in with a vengeance.

As I opened the front door, I saw my gran lying flat on her back in the hallway. Her stiffened fingers clutched at her chest and her pale glassy eyes stared sightlessly back into mine. *A heart attack*, the paramedic said when he finally got up the sixteen flights of stairs. *We'll have to let your parents know*.

As they wheeled her body out of the front door, I sat there alone in the flat. From the street outside, I could hear the sound of shouts and breaking glass. I felt numb, but I knew what I had to do. It was time to go. Heading back into school, I walked into the computer suite for the final time. I was ready to put my plan into action.

First of all, I wiped out every trace of Harrison Andrews: my birth certificate, medical records, mobile-phone statements, bank-account details. From the school network to government databases, I didn't leave a single byte of data behind. It was as if Harrison Andrews had never existed.

And in his place, I built a new life for myself. I chose a new name – Luke Kitson. I've always been tall for my age, so I just added a few extra years to Luke's birth certificate to make myself eighteen years old. After all, life's easier when you're a grown-up, right? And to give myself the best possible start to my new life, I gave Luke straight A* exam results and a multi-million-pound trust fund.

Don't worry, I didn't steal it. That's all money is nowadays – just a string of ones and zeroes floating in cyberspace. With the right program, I could put a million pounds in your bank account tomorrow and nobody would be any the wiser. I'd show you how, but like I said, trade secrets.

While the ICT teacher sat at his desk marking a pile of essays, I uploaded my photograph to Luke Kitson's online records. I watched the picture as it appeared on the screen – my piercing blue eyes staring out distrustfully from beneath a fringe of dark-brown hair. Beneath the ID photo was my new name and date of birth. The transformation was complete.

Before I logged off the computer, I used my new bank account to book myself on to the next train down to London – first class, of course. Then I walked out of the classroom and into my new life.

That was only six months ago, but as I looked out of the window on to the city below, I still couldn't quite believe it.

I flopped down on the sofa as the roar of the crowd swelled from the speakers, ready to watch the second half of the match. Sitting in front of my giant 3D TV screen, I had the best seat in the stadium. As Chelsea kicked off, there was the distant sound of a knock at the door. I ignored it. The whole suite of apartments was security coded. Nobody could even get to my front door without my buzzing them in on the video intercom. It must just be one of the maintenance guys who had taken a wrong turn.

The knocking started again, heavier this time. Irritated, I peeled myself off the sofa as Arsenal broke down the right. As I headed towards the apartment door, the roar of the crowd grew louder. Getting ready to give the guy a piece of my mind, I keyed in the security code and the front door swung open.

Standing there was a tall man in a sharp suit. His dark hair was closely cropped, and his eyes shaded behind sunglasses.

'Hello, Harrison,' he said with a knowing smile.

The name hit me like a punch to the gut. *Harrison Andrews*. The boy I thought I had left behind. I stared anxiously back at my reflection in his mirrored shades, my face suddenly pale.

'Mind if I come in?' the man asked.

CHAPTER TWO

'My name's not Harrison – it's Luke.'

I could barely get the words out of my mouth as the harsh thudding of my heart swelled and filled my throat.

The man shook his head.

'We know who you are, Harrison,' he replied briskly, brushing past me as he stepped inside the apartment, 'but if you prefer it, I'll call you Luke.'

He walked along the entrance hall, trailing his finger along the polished chrome fittings that lined it. In a daze I followed him, my mind racing in fear.

Reaching the large open-plan living space, the man glanced around at the gadgets strewn about the place. On the big screen, the match still blared from the speakers. The roar of the crowd was almost deafening as the blue shirts of Chelsea piled forward on the attack. He pulled his mobile phone out from his pocket and waved it once in the direction of the screen. In an instant, the TV snapped into silence and the screen faded to black.

The man turned towards me. Through the windows that stretched from floor to ceiling, the city skyline framed his imposing figure.

'Nice place you've got here,' he said with a tone of grudging admiration in his voice. 'Must be worth a couple of million, at least – and that's without all the gear you've got stashed away in here. Now, how can a fourteen-year-old boy afford all this?'

A bead of sweat rolled down my face. In my chest, I could feel the pounding of my heart quickening as I met the man's inscrutable gaze. Who was he? The smartly tailored suit was far too flash for any policeman, while nobody at the bank I had hacked into would be clever enough to find my digital fingerprints on their hard drives.

'I don't know what you're talking about,' I blustered. 'You've got me mixed up with someone else. I'm eighteen years old – I paid for all this myself. I've got a trust fund –'

The man waved me into silence with a dismissive flick of his wrist. He slowly removed his sunglasses and I saw for the first time the cold blue steel in his stare.

'You're tall for your age,' he replied, casting his eyes over me with a critical gaze. 'I'll give you that. That'll come in handy later on. But don't think you can bluff your way out of this. You see, we've been watching you, *Luke* – we know exactly what you've done. Hacking into government computers, wiping encrypted database records, cracking open new identity files. You even infiltrated one of the tightest bank security systems ever built to set yourself up a multi-million-pound account.' A thin-lipped smile tightened his face. 'You're good. If it hadn't been for a few schoolboy errors, we'd never have been able to track you down.'

I felt my cheeks redden as the man's gaze almost burned through me. *A few schoolboy errors* ... From outside the window came a low rumble of thunder and drops of rain began to splatter against the glass. This was it. It was all over. The new life I'd created for myself was going to be taken away before I'd even had the chance to start living it.

'Your work shows promise,' the man continued. 'A little raw, perhaps, but we can we work on that. We've been looking for someone with your particular skills for quite some time. That's why I've come here today – to ask you to join us.'

I stood there dumbfounded, my mind spinning as a barrage of questions and fears tumbled around my brain. But among the man's words, a faint ray of hope shone through the gloom. *Ask you to join us.*

'What do you mean?' I asked him, fighting to keep the tremor out of my voice. 'Who are you?'

The man held out his hand in greeting.

'Elliot Carter,' he replied, grasping my hand with a powerful grip. 'I'm the head of the Elite.'

Wincing as I pulled my fingers free from his handshake, I stared up into the man's stern features. His chiselled face was set in a deadpan expression; eyes unblinking in an unshakeable stare. What on earth was he talking about?

'The Elite?' I asked, struggling to make sense of the name. 'Who are they?'

'The Elite are a covert division of the secret service,' Elliot explained. 'Electronic Intelligence Tracking and

Elimination. We are this country's first and last line of defence against the countless digital threats that we face every day. Spies hacking into military websites. Environmental extremists sabotaging nuclear power-plant systems. Cyberterrorists plotting all-out attacks against the nation itself. The Elite is there to combat these threats and fight back against our attackers.'

I couldn't stop myself from laughing. The idea was ridiculous.

'You must be joking.'

The fear that had been running through my veins from the moment Elliot Carter had appeared at my door was fading fast. 'You want me to become a cyber-spy?'

The humourless expression fixed to Elliot's face didn't even flicker.

'We prefer the term "Cyberspace Intelligence Agents",' he replied. 'And don't think you're the first. The Elite has recruited other naughty boys like you. We find we can put your talents to much better use.'

I stared at him in disbelief. Did he expect me to believe this nonsense? I shook my head.

'No thanks,' I replied, 'I think I'll stick to playing spy games on my games console.'

I sat back down on the sofa. Reaching for the remote control, I flicked the TV on again.

'Now, if you don't mind leaving me in peace, I'd like to get on with watching the match.'

Frowning, Elliot waved his mobile phone in the direction of the TV again. The football match disappeared in a storm of static before the screen turned black.

'Don't be too hasty.' His voice sharpened with a note of warning, 'Take a look at this first.'

He held out the mobile towards me and I reluctantly took hold of it. On the screen, I saw an open list of files. Archived web pages, Internet service logs, financial records and video files. Flicking through each file, I could see every detail of my plan to transform myself from Harrison Andrews to Luke Kitson captured forever. Every website that I'd hacked, my every move tracked. On this mobile was an avalanche of evidence that could bury me forever.

In the last video clip, I saw CCTV pictures showing me withdrawing a bundle of notes from a nearby cashpoint. The balance of my bank account could be seen on the screen: a cool two million pounds.

I glanced up at Elliot Carter with the sense of fear returning. His nerveless smile told me what I knew already. He had me trapped.

'Like I said, we've been watching you for a long time, Luke.' Elliot calmly plucked his mobile phone from my fingers. 'I think the Metropolitan Police would be very interested to see all of this,' he continued, before finally putting his warning into words. 'Unauthorized access to protected computers, identity theft, banking fraud – you'd be looking at a minimum ten-year stretch in prison.'

A cold shiver of dread ran down my spine, fixing me to my seat. Frozen, I watched as Elliot turned his back on me and stared out through the window. Rain was now falling in sheets across the city. The skyline that only minutes before had been bathed in sunlight was now dirty and grey.

'So, what's it going to be?' Elliot asked, his eyes still fixed to the horizon. 'Are you going to waste your talents locked away in some tiny cell where you'll never see a computer again, or are you going to join the Elite?'

I fought to keep a wave of nausea at bay. There was no way out. When I finally managed to reply, my answer almost stuck in my throat.

'It doesn't look like I've got any choice, does it?'

CHAPTER THREE

'Where are you taking me?' I asked Elliot as we walked along the Embankment. On the far side of the River Thames, a low cluster of government buildings huddled beneath a slate-grey sky. 'MI5? MI6? The Ministry of Defence? Who exactly runs this Elite?'

Glancing towards me, Elliot's face hardened.

'I do,' he replied. 'In the security services, MI5 only combats conventional threats to national security from inside the UK, while MI6 deals with matters of overseas intelligence. The Elite knows no boundaries. The Internet is global and so are we. We don't take orders from MI5 or MI6 – we give them orders when we need their particular assistance. Any digital threat to the security of this nation comes under my command.' He shook his head with a wry smile. 'As for those chinless wonders at the Ministry of Defence, the only time we pick up the phone to them is when we need something blowing up.'

My mind whirred as it processed the information – a secret team of cyber-spooks protecting the country. I looked across at Elliot as he strode grimly on.

'So, why have you chosen me then?' I pressed. 'I'm just a kid. Surely, you've got enough real spies to keep the country safe from computer attack?'

Elliot's brow furrowed in response to the question. 'It takes on average three months to train an Elite agent,' he replied. 'In that time, the technological tactics that terrorists use to attack this country will have changed at least a thousand times. Every day brings a new kind of threat. The digital world is fast-moving. Most adults can't cope – their minds are analogue. But your generation was born digital. The teenage mind learns faster, makes connections more quickly. All the skills an Elite agent needs.'

As we walked, his gaze flicked over me again, sizing me up.

'I've told you, Luke – we only recruit the best. You've already proved you've got potential – cracking into government websites, deleting encrypted files, creating your new identity. All that will come in handy in your role as an Elite agent.' The faint hint of a smile played round the edges of his mouth. 'Set a thief to catch a thief, as the old saying goes.'

Elliot turned left off the Embankment, leaving the broad expanse of the Thames behind. As he led me down a gloomy side street, I hurried to keep up. The narrow street ran beneath a railway arch, graffiti tags sprayed across the shop-fronts and boarded-up windows. A short cut, I thought, to somewhere more exciting.

The worries that had been nagging away at me were gone now, replaced with a growing sense of anticipation. If this was for real, then I was going to have the chance to become a digital James Bond. I felt an expectant smile creep across my face. Maybe I'd even get my own Aston Martin equipped with the latest hi-tech gadgets.

'So, where *are* we going to?' I asked again.

Elliot stopped outside a second-hand electronics shop. Its grimy windows were plastered with phone cards and peeling handwritten signs. Behind these, I could see piles of electronic clutter: ancient video-game consoles, grubby laptops, battery chargers and brick-like mobile phones. Every single piece of kit looked at least ten years out of date.

'The centre of our operations,' Elliot replied, pushing open the shop door and gesturing for me to follow him inside. 'Elite HQ.'

I stared at him as if he was insane.

'You're joking, right?'

Elliot shook his head, his face a stern mask of certainty.

'I don't joke when the security of our nation is at stake,' he said gruffly. 'Now follow me.'

Frowning, I followed Elliot inside. The bell above the shop door tinkled faintly as we stepped across the threshold. As I looked around, my dreams of a custom-built Aston Martin crumbled to dust.

The shop shelves were littered with mounds of junk. Beaten-up radios and wireless routers. Satellite dishes and stacks of printer cartridges. It looked like an electronics graveyard – a place where technology came to die.

At the back of the shop, I saw a burly man leaning against the counter. His dark hair was scraped back into a lank ponytail and a greying goatee beard perched on his chin. He was leafing through the pages of a newspaper, yesterday's football results spread out in front of him.

He glanced up as Elliot approached the counter.

'Can I help you, sir?' he asked, folding the newspaper away. 'Are you looking for anything in particular?'

Elliot nodded. 'My TV isn't working,' he replied. 'I need a new system – 3D LED TV, high-definition screen, integrated Blu-ray and hard-drive recorder.'

Nodding his head in return, the man lifted a flap in the counter for Elliot.

'I believe we have what you're looking for in the back storeroom,' he said, 'if you'd like to go through.'

As Elliot eased his way past the counter, I shook my head in confusion. Everything on the shelves in here looked like junk, but they kept state-of-the-art equipment like that out of sight in their stockroom?

'Come on, Luke.'

The bark of Elliot's voice snapped me out of my surprise. In a daze, I followed him behind the counter. The shopkeeper eyed me suspiciously as I passed him, his beady gaze tracking my path as I picked my way through coils of cables and connectors.

Elliot seemed to know exactly where he was going as he pushed open a door at the back of the shop. He led me down a narrow corridor littered with boxes of electronic equipment. My trainers stuck to the threadbare carpet as I skirted a box of leaking batteries. An acrid smell clung to the walls.

'I thought you were taking me to the Elite HQ,' I said to Elliot with a scowl, unable to keep the irritation out of my voice. 'Not buying yourself a new TV.'

Ahead of us, the corridor came to an end. Stacks of cardboard boxes were piled up against the wall. Elliot shoved these to one side to reveal a lift door hidden behind. Pushing the call button, the door slid open and he turned towards me with thin-lipped smile.

'You'll see,' he said. 'Get in.'

Muttering crossly under my breath, I climbed into the cramped lift with Elliot following close behind. As the lift door slid shut with a clang, Elliot reached towards the control panel with his mobile phone in his hand. Pressing the phone against the panel, it buzzed once in acknowledgement and then the lift began to slowly judder downwards.

'What's that?'

'Encrypted Bluetooth security key,' Elliot replied as he pocketed his mobile. 'Only an Elite agent would be able to get this lift to move.'

Leaning against the wall of the lift, I felt the smooth steel shell vibrate as we descended. On the control panel, I saw the light behind the button marked 'Basement' blink out of existence, but the lift continued to judder its way downwards. Ten, fifteen, twenty seconds passed as we headed deeper underground.

I glanced over at Elliot again. His face was expressionless as he stared straight ahead. The flame of doubt inside my mind began to flicker. How did I know if he was even telling the truth? Where was he really taking me? As the lift continued to descend, a cold line of sweat trickled down my back. If I disappeared, nobody would ever know. Only my gran had ever cared and she was gone now. My pulse rate began to quicken at the thought of what could be waiting for me when we reached the bottom.

Without warning, the lift shuddered to a halt. A razor-thin sliver of light was visible in the gap between the door and the wall. In the room beyond, silence waited.

Elliot lifted his head and stared up at a point just above the lift door. Following his gaze, I could see a small circular glint of light – the tell-tale sign of a hidden camera lens.

'It's Carter,' he said, addressing the camera. 'I'm back and I've brought our latest recruit.'

As if in reply, the door slid open. Elliot stepped forward and I reluctantly followed him out of the lift. I stopped dead, my neck swivelling in wonder as I scoped out my surroundings.

We were standing in a vast open-plan workspace. Its pristine white ceiling arced above me. On the walls, huge plasma screens showed maps of the world, its countries and cities overlaid with pulsing dots and scrolling data. Security briefings, intelligence warnings, threat levels. The maps were constantly updating with a blizzard of information.

Beneath these screens, a cluster of sleek workstations were positioned in the centre of the room. Seated there, a trio of teenagers glanced up as Elliot strode across the polished floor. He turned back towards me as I stood there frozen, my mouth hanging open in amazement.

'Welcome to the Elite.'

CHAPTER FOUR

'This is where we save the country every single day.'

Dumbfounded, I followed Elliot as he led me towards the heart of the room. He gestured towards the huge plasma screens. On these, a constellation of flashing lights pulsed across the globe and a constant stream of data scrolled in front of my eyes.

'These maps show the major cyber-threats the United Kingdom is currently facing. Spyware launched by rogue agents, Trojan horses sent by enemy states, malicious viruses spread by terrorist splinter groups. Each one of those flashing dots pinpoints exactly where in the world the attack has come from.'

Elliot reached the central hub of workstations and rested his hands on the back of an empty chair. At the other desks, the three teenagers – two boys and one girl – sat with their eyes fixed to their flat-screen monitors, their fingers racing across wireless keyboards.

'The Elite agents in this room are the firewall that protects the rest of the nation. It's their job to stop these cyber-attacks and fight back against the invisible enemies that plague us. Come on, I want you to meet the team.'

He motioned towards the figure sitting in front of the nearest computer. I looked across to see a girl, a couple of years younger than me, maybe, her face pale in the digitally generated glow. The headset she was wearing framed a pixie cut of dyed-red hair, and her green eyes darted across a double-row of six computer screens set round her keyboard.

On each screen, I could see a blur of social networking sites, webcasts and blog feeds. Digital conversations were constantly updating as volleys of instant messages popped in and out of existence. It was information overload – just looking at a single screen made my head ache.

'This is Angela,' Elliot said. 'She's in charge of our social networking surveillance.'

The girl glanced up and nodded in acknowledgement, her fingers not even pausing for a second as they danced across the keyboard.

'Sorry, can't talk,' she explained, noisily chewing gum as she spoke. She glanced across at Elliot. 'I think I'm close to a breakthrough on the undercover Krasnian cell. They're plotting something – something big.'

A grim smile of satisfaction broke across Elliot's face.

'Good work,' he told her. 'Let me know when you find out exactly what it is they're planning and we can make the necessary arrangements.'

Still chewing, Angela nodded her head and turned back to her bank of monitors.

Elliot lowered his voice as he led me round the central hub towards the next workstation.

'The Elite monitoring system handles over two million messages every hour. Status updates, blog posts, emails and tweets. We search these for any possible threats to our national security. Most of the messages we intercept are harmless and automatically filtered out by our software. But if a message contains a code word that we are monitoring, then it is flagged on the database for analysis.'

'What, you mean every time I post anything online you're reading what I write? That's outrageous!'

Elliot frowned.

'If you're not doing anything you shouldn't be doing, then you don't have anything to worry about,' he replied coldly. 'It's not kids posting photos of their Friday nights out we're interested in. Terrorist organisations and extremist groups have started using these social networks to organise their plans. At the moment, Angela is infiltrating a radical group of extremists from the rogue state of Krasnia. They're using social networking sites to organise an attack on UK soil. Thousands of lives are at stake unless she finds out exactly where and when they plan to strike.'

I glanced back at Angela. She was still chewing noisily, her mouth hanging open in concentration as the wireless mouse beneath her hand arced across the desk.

'But she's just a kid!'

'And that's what makes her the best,' Elliot replied. 'She's been using these social networks since she was a toddler. She won the Webby award for best social networker three years in a row before her tenth birthday. The mobile-blogging company she set up with her father turned over ten million pounds in its first year. It's only our good fortune that Angela decided to put her special talents in the service of her country instead.'

Elliot came to a halt in front of the two teenage boys. They were sat facing each other, both tapping away at matching white laptops. An array of discarded USB sticks, memory cards and external hard drives littered the desk between them.

'Unlike these two,' he said. 'Like you, they needed a little more persuasion to join the Elite. Luke, meet Rez and Jimi – our in-house hacking team.'

The two boys looked up and I saw, with a jolt of surprise, the same face staring back at me twice. Messy fringes of dark, lank hair fell across their foreheads and, beneath these, identical pairs of piercing brown eyes met my gaze. The two boys were both dressed entirely in black. It was impossible to tell them apart.

'All right,' they replied in unison. 'So you're the latest recruit.'

I nodded my head dumbly. On the giant screens above, a scrolling message began to flash red – threat level: SEVERE. My mind was still spinning with what I had learned. It was true. Great Britain was protected from cyber-attack by a handful of teenagers.

'I recruited Rez and Jimi myself,' Elliot continued, oblivious to the warning flashing above his head. 'They hacked into the Ministry of Defence's secure mainframes for a laugh and ended up ordering enough military equipment to start World War Three. It was only after they turned up to school in a tank that I managed to track them down. With a little retraining, they both found that their expertise could be used more effectively on our side of the computer screen.'

I stifled a grin as, behind Elliot's back, both Rez and Jimi mimed exaggerated yawns. Seeing the expression on my face, Elliot frowned, his tone hardening as he began to speak again.

'And with the right training, I'm sure that you can be just as useful to us, Luke,' he said. 'But you'll need to learn fast. We don't carry any passengers in the Elite.'

I felt my cheeks redden at his warning, an embarrassed blush rising from my neck.

'There's one last member of the team you still need to meet,' Elliot continued. 'A veteran agent who's been with the Elite from the moment the organisation was first formed.'

From the far side of the cavernous space, a door slid open. Turning my head, I saw a teenage girl striding across the floor towards us. She was wearing black combat trousers and a green hooded top embroidered with the slogan *DOWNLOADING THE FUTURE*. Her blonde bobbed hair was clipped back from her face, which was momentarily hidden in the pages of a print-out. As she looked up, I saw that she was around sixteen years old and drop-dead gorgeous. For a second our eyes met, but then she quickly looked away, her striking features set in a hard-faced scowl.

'This is Gemma Deal,' Elliot began, 'otherwise known as Gems. Gemma, let me introduce you to Luke Kitson – our latest recruit.'

Slamming herself down in front of an empty workstation, Gemma waved Elliot into silence. She flung the print-out across the desk towards him.

'There's no time for introductions,' she replied, her fingers racing across the computer keyboard. 'The UK is under attack.'

CHAPTER FIVE

'One hour ago, every online video-game service in Britain received the following message.'

As Elliot read the email print-out in his hand, Gemma clicked on her mouse and the same message flashed up on the huge plasma screen directly above my head.

From: Angry Parents United
To: CEO@GameSector Network
Subject: Game Over

Attention, Timewasters! You have been found guilty of crimes against homework. In the name of all parents who battle every night to drag their children away from the video-game console, we hereby sentence you to extinction. You have sixty minutes left until we turn out the lights. Get ready to meet the ultimate end-of-level boss!

'The video-game companies thought it was just a hoax,' Gemma continued, her fingers frantically tapping away. 'Some joker trying to scare them into shutting down. But to make sure, their in-house security teams checked that their servers were safe from any kind of cyber-attack. Firewalls reinstalled, passwords changed, anti-virus software updated.

There should have been no way for any hackers to crack their systems.'

Gemma glanced up and I noticed for the first time a glint of doubt in her dark-blue eyes.

'Then five minutes ago, the GameSector Network website came under attack. A worm burrowed its way into the company's mainframe computer, dodging past every security program in place. Once inside, it started deleting user accounts and transferring their gamer credits to an unknown destination. Then it started to wipe the code of every single video game on the network. Adventure games, sports simulators, first-person shooters – they were all infected. In less than a minute, the GameSector Network website was completely destroyed.' She shook her head in disbelief. 'There's just an empty hole in cyberspace where it used to be.'

I winced at the thought of that mindless destruction. After school, I used to log on to the GameSector Network nearly every night. Teaming up with my friends online, we'd battle it out playing the hottest new releases. For a year, my name headed every leader board until the network banned me from playing. They said they wanted to give other users a chance of hitting the top spot. My face tightened into a scowl. Those were my gamer credits disappearing into the depths of cyberspace!

'The same worm is now attacking every online gaming service in Britain,' Gemma continued. 'Their security systems are crumbling. If we don't stop it soon, the whole of the UK video-game industry could go under.'

Gemma paused for a moment as if awaiting her orders. The clouds gathering across Elliot's face had darkened. His brow furrowed as he worked out their next move. Then with a flurry of orders, he snapped into action.

'Gems – get me every online gaming service up on screen now.'

'I'm already on it,' she replied. With a click of her mouse, a complex grid of interconnected networks filled the huge plasma screen. Flickering routes and pathways pulsed between the hubs of the gaming services. Each one showed the flow of online players around the system.

'Rez, Jimi,' Elliot barked. 'I want you to track down where these attacks are coming from. We need to cut this worm off at the source.'

Swiftly nodding their heads in unison, the twins bent over their laptops. Elliot turned towards Angela who was wrenching off her headset with one hand as she typed furiously with the other.

'Angela – find out who's behind this. Run a full spectrum sweep of the Elite monitoring system and all social networking feeds. Look for any mention of planned attacks against the gaming industry. Round up the usual suspects – rogue hackers, unemployed programmers, disgruntled teachers. I want to know who Angry Parents United really is.'

As the team whirled into action, I stood there open-mouthed. The speed of events was dizzying. On the plasma screen overhead, the pulsing pathways began to turn from green to red. One by one, the gaming networks began to fall.

'What should I do?' I asked as Elliot hovered over Gemma's shoulder. His face was grim as he watched her fingers dance across the keyboard, frantically trying to deactivate the worm as it spread like a virus across the system.

'This is no time for beginner's on-the-job training,' he growled, keeping his eyes fixed to the screen. 'Just keep out of the way and watch.'

I felt a hot flush of indignation rising in my chest. *No time for beginners.* I hadn't come here to be treated like a kid. I probably knew more about these online games networks than the rest of them put together. After all, I'd managed to bypass their security programs myself. It was the only way I'd been able to carry on playing whenever the games networks tried to kick me off their servers for being too good.

'I thought you were here to protect national security,' I grumbled. 'You can't even stop a bunch of video-game companies from being taken down. What's the big deal anyway? It's not like they're that important.'

Elliot looked up with a scowl.

'Who do you think owns these companies? Every major government in the world runs their own network of online video-game services. This is a direct attack on the United Kingdom's network.'

I stared at him incredulous.

'That's crazy. Why?'

'It's where we train our armed forces. First-person shooters, combat simulators, stealth games and strategy. These video games equip our army, navy and air force personnel with the front-line skills they need without the risk of any collateral damage. The entire network is funded from the government defence budget.'

I couldn't believe what he was telling me. 'What about all the other games?' I asked, shaking my head in disbelief. 'How's getting a high score on *Guitar Hero* going to help you in a war zone?'

'R & R – rest and relaxation,' Elliot replied. 'Even the toughest soldier needs to unwind.'

'But I used to log on and play these games – all the kids at school did.'

'I know,' Elliot replied with a thin-lipped smile. 'The UK's online games network has proved very useful in helping the Ministry of Defence to identify and recruit a new generation of soldiers. If this worm manages to take the network down, it'll blow a massive hole in the UK's military training and recruitment programmes. The armed forces might never recover.' He turned back to the computer screen. 'Now keep quiet and let us get on with stopping it.'

On the giant plasma screen, I watched as several of the smaller hubs pulsed with a crimson glow. The network of pathways spinning off them like the spokes of a wheel started to run red.

Gemma glanced up, her fingers still racing across the keyboard.

'It's picking off the gaming services with the weakest security systems first. Half of the combat and war games are down – we've just lost the army's sniper training system.'

'Kill it,' Elliot growled, gripping the back of her chair. 'I want that worm destroyed.'

Gemma shook her head in frustration. 'I'm throwing everything we've got at it, but it's invulnerable to attack. I've never seen a virus like it – it's an Apocalypse Worm. Every time it takes control of one network's computer servers it sends an army of clones to attack the others. The more it destroys, the stronger it gets.'

On the screen I saw three more of the game hubs begin to glow red, their infected tentacles creeping beyond our shores.

'The worm's going global now. It's attacking online video-game networks in Russia and China. Their defences are holding firm for the moment, but it's only a matter of time until the worm breaks through.'

Elliot's mouth twisted in an angry snarl.

'If it manages to infiltrate their systems, those countries will think it's an act of war. We've got to stop it now!'

He turned back towards the twins.

'Rez, Jimi – tell me where these attacks are coming from. We have to shut them down.'

Glancing up, the two brothers exchanged worried glances. Rez shook his head as Jimi hammered his fingers against his laptop keyboard.

'They're coming from everywhere. Simultaneous attacks from Internet cafes, school ICT suites and Wi-Fi hotspots. The worm's growing with every new attack. Now it's inside the system there's no way to stop it spreading. We've only got a couple of minutes until it wipes the Russian and Chinese networks off the map.'

Rez's words hung in the air. Two minutes until apocalypse.

CHAPTER SIX

Elliot drummed his fists against the back of an empty workstation. His gaze flicked to each of the team in turn.

'There's got to be a way that we can stop it,' he growled. 'Come on, how can we kill this worm before it starts World War Three?'

My mind raced as I stared up at the giant plasma screen. As I watched the worm burrowing through the system, the pathways glowing red where it passed, the spark of an idea caught fire in my mind. It was travelling too fast now for us to stop it, replicating itself with incredible speed, but if we could make it come to us ...

I turned back to Elliot.

'We can't kill it,' I told him, 'but we can trap it.'

Elliot stared at me in surprise.

'What do you mean?'

I quickly stepped over to the empty workstation. Slipping in front of the computer there, I quickly patched it into the mainframe. The same pulsing grid of pathways appeared on my screen. Grabbing a memory stick, I jabbed it into the computer's USB port.

'This Apocalypse Worm has been programmed with one goal,' I explained, my fingers rattling a chain of commands into the keyboard as I spoke. 'It won't stop until it has taken down every online games service in the world. But if we shut them down first, then the worm won't have anywhere left to go.'

Elliot groaned in disappointment.

'How's that going to help us? If we try to shut down the Russian and Chinese networks – they'll think we are behind the attack. And what for? The worm will just hibernate and as soon as their servers are switched on again, they'll be toast.'

I shook my head.

'We only have to shut them down for a split second – just long enough to bring the worm to us.'

Elliot narrowed his eyes.

'What do you mean?'

I turned towards Gemma. She was staring back at me intrigued, a faint flicker of hope shining in her eyes.

'Can you create a mirror site on the Elite mainframe computer of one of the gaming sites that hasn't yet been infected?'

Gemma nodded.

'I just need to clone the system files – it should only take a minute.'

'Make it seconds,' I told her, 'and we might have a chance of stopping this.'

In reply, Gemma's fingers raced across the keyboard. Her eyes flicked back and forth as scrolling patterns of indecipherable text rolled across the screen; the computer unquestioningly carrying out her commands. After ten short seconds that felt like an hour, she glanced up at me with a swift nod of her head.

'It's done.'

'Wait a minute,' Elliot's voice rose in protest. 'This is crazy – there's no way we can let that worm anywhere near our systems. Think about the damage it would wreak.'

'It won't have the chance.' I rapped my knuckles against the side of my computer. 'When the networks are shut down for a split second, our mirror site will fool the worm into thinking that we are the last video-gaming service left standing. If we route its access point through this one machine, then we can trap the worm before it even reaches the mainframe.'

Deep lines of worry creased Elliot's forehead.

'If you've got this wrong –'

His warning was cut off by Rez's anxious countdown.

'One minute left.'

'It's our only chance,' said Gemma, her voice taut with urgency. 'Just give me the order.'

With a pained sigh, Elliot nodded his head.

'Gems, get ready to shut the networks down on Luke's command. For a split second only.' He fixed me with a cold-eyed stare. 'I hope you know what you're doing.'

Breaking his gaze, my eyes flicked down to the computer screen. I could feel the familiar rush of excitement pulsing through my veins. My fingers flew across the keyboard, setting the trap in place. One last command and it was ready.

Glancing up, my eyes met Gemma's and I saw the same reckless spark that beat in my veins reflected in her eyes. 'Now!'

On the giant plasma screen, the shimmering grid flickered out of life. At the same instant, a mirror image sprung into life on my computer. The network's flickering routes and pathways were now almost completely engulfed by a pulsing red tide. The worm turned, heading for the one green hub remaining on the screen – the Elite mainframe. In less than a second it would be inside.

I only had the one chance to get this right. As the router flashed, I snatched the memory stick out of the drive.

The image of the pulsing network froze on my computer screen. Then, on the giant plasma overhead, the grid of video-game networks spanning the world flickered back into life. Looking up, I breathed out a loud sigh of relief as I saw the pathways glowing green once more. The worm was gone.

As the team broke into cheers, I brandished the memory stick with a grin. The LED light on its side flashed red – the Apocalypse Worm imprisoned inside.

'Nicely done,' said Gemma, the grin on her face as wide as my own. 'You're an i-ssassin now.'

CHAPTER SEVEN

The next few weeks passed by in a whirl of training as I learned the secrets of the Elite. Shadowing my fellow agents, I watched as they showed me how to hack into terrorist communications systems, trail and terminate the identities of enemy spies, and infiltrate the electronic underground that lurked beneath the surface of the Internet.

It was the ultimate thrill. To an outsider, we just looked like a bunch of kids sitting in front of a computer screen. But every day I learned how to battle invisible enemies using every weapon at my command.

Angela taught me how to hijack suspects' social networking accounts. It bugged me at first being trained by a girl who was barely out of primary school. But I soon forgot about that as she showed me the surveillance tools that Elite agents used. With a click of a mouse, I could eavesdrop on your emails and instant messages, install spyware on your phone and home computer, read every update that you post. In less than a few minutes, I would know everything about you – your biggest secrets, your darkest fears.

Rez and Jimi supervised the upgrade to my hacking skills. *We're the masters of unauthorized access*, they told me with a grin. *There's not a computer system we haven't cracked yet.* From the Kremlin to the Pentagon, the mainframes of huge multinational corporations to the computer sitting on your desk, the twins could get inside it. They treated it like a game and the World Wide Web was their playground as they showed me the tricks of their trade. I learned fast. In the digital world there were no limits.

As for Gemma, I just watched her in awe. Elliot was in charge, but she led the team on most of our missions. Working together, we busted a gang of criminals who were trying to wipe the police database, located a captured MI6 agent in the heart of enemy territory, and defended the UK's military satellites from cyber-attack. Whatever the threat, her ice-cool calm never flickered.

As well as our minds, Elliot pushed us to train our bodies too. *Keeping fit boosts your brain power*, he told us. *To be an Elite agent you need to be at the top of your game.* In the gymnasium beneath Elite HQ, I gasped for breath as I struggled to keep pace with the rest of the team. Rez and Jimi pounded out the miles on parallel running machines, music blaring through their headphones. On a nearby cross-trainer, Gemma stared up at a TV screen showing the constant stream of data reports rolling into the Elite monitoring system. With beads of sweat rolling down her face, Gems kept a close eye on any cyber-threats even as she pushed her body to the limit.

Climbing down from my exercise bike, I watched as Angela practised her martial arts moves on the exercise mat. I'd been to a few tae kwon do classes myself back at school. The trainer had told me that I had a natural talent for it. Maybe it was time I showed the others what I was really capable of.

'Need a sparring partner?' I asked.

Glancing up, Angela shook her head.

'I don't think that would be a good idea,' she replied. 'I don't want to hurt you.'

I stared at her in disbelief. She was three years younger and thirty centimetres shorter than me. She wouldn't have a chance of getting near me, let alone getting in a blow.

On the cross-trainer behind Angela, I saw Gemma glance across and smile. My own cheeks reddened. I couldn't lose face like this.

'Come on,' I badgered Angela. 'I'll take it easy on you – I promise.'

Raising an eyebrow beneath her pixie-red fringe, she slowly sighed in reply.

'It's your funeral.'

Facing each other across the mat, we exchanged a short bow. My mind buzzed with the tae kwon do moves I remembered from my training. It'd be a piece of cake to take her down a peg or two.

Without warning, I launched myself at Angela across the mat. A spinning kick aiming to sweep her legs from under her. But my kick found empty air as Angela dodged past the strike with lightning speed. Turning in confusion, I unleashed another attack. My feet and fists flew as I tried to find a way past Angela's defences. But she effortlessly blocked my every move.

To Gemma, Rez and Jimi who were now watching on with interest, it looked like some kind of desperate ballet. My lunging strikes and sweeping kicks were counterpointed by Angela's graceful evasions, her arms and legs a blur as she warded off every blow.

Breathing heavily, I circled her warily.

'Don't worry.' Angela smiled, her green eyes glittering mischievously. 'I'll take it easy on you.'

With these words, she sprang forward. Ducking past my defences, her outstretched hand slammed into my stomach. The hammer blow from her fist forced the breath from my body and I crumpled to the floor.

As I lay there, gasping for air, Angela stood over me. Her face was creased with concern and she reached down towards me with an open hand.

'I'm sorry,' she said as she helped pull me to my feet. 'I should have warned you that I'm a ninth dan.'

I winced in realisation. That made her a black belt – a martial arts grand master. No wonder she'd kicked my butt. The smiles on the faces of the others told me that I wasn't the first to fall victim to Angela's flying fists.

That night when I got back to my apartment, I lay on the bed staring up at the ceiling. The fresh bruise across my stomach still ached, but it couldn't mask the worries that crowded my mind. What had happened today showed me how far I still had to go to make it as an Elite agent. The others didn't say anything, but I knew that I was still on probation. Any mistake and Elliot would ship me off back to my old life as Harrison Andrews.

Just thinking about this reminded me how alone I was. Every single day I tried to put any thoughts of my old life out of my mind. The memories of my gran were lost in the whirlwind of excitement and danger at the heart of the Elite. How I wished she was here now.

I turned on to my side, trying to get comfortable. I couldn't sleep as my brain reeled with everything I had learned. Through the open blinds, London's night skyline illuminated my bedroom with a faint orange glow, but I could only see the flickering streams of data that filled my mind. And I wanted to know more. I wanted to be the best Elite agent there had ever been.

CHAPTER EIGHT

Early the next morning, Elliot called me into his office. He was standing in front of a long glass window that looked out on the central hub. Over his shoulder, I could see Gemma, Rez and Jimi crowded round one of the workstation computers, a video game filling its display. The huge plasma screens were quiet for once – the current threat level warning downgraded to low.

As the office door slid closed behind me, Elliot turned and gestured to an empty chair in front of his desk. Sitting down, I racked my brain for the reason that he'd called me in. Lowering his broad frame into his leather chair, Elliot tapped at the keys of a silver laptop that lay open on the desk between us.

'I have been watching your progress with interest, Luke.'

As he spoke, I couldn't stop a small confident smile creeping across my lips. Maybe Gemma had told Elliot about how I'd helped foil an extremist attack earlier that week by hacking into the gang's satnav and redirecting their van to MI5 headquarters.

'Behind a computer keyboard you've proved yourself,' he continued, 'but there's more to being an Elite agent than just hiding away in here.'

The confident smile quickly faded from my face. I looked at him quizzically, my brow furrowed beneath a cloud of doubt.

Elliot's face was set in its usual stern frown. 'I think you're ready for the next step,' he said. 'It's time for you to take on your first field mission.'

The clouds that had been gathering across my face lifted. This was it – the moment I'd been waiting for. It'd been all very well learning the ropes from the others, but now I had the chance to stand on my own two feet. I couldn't wait to get started.

'What do you want me to do?' I asked eagerly. 'Is it an enemy agent you want me to follow? A terrorist cell you need me to crack?'

Elliot held up his open palm to silence me.

'Patience,' he replied. 'Angela will brief you on the details. She's taking charge of this mission.'

Behind me, I heard the door slide open and Angela slipped into the chair next to mine. I glanced across to see her green eyes sparkling beneath her short spiky fringe.

'So you're ready to hit the streets then?' she asked.

I slowly nodded my head, trying to hide the disappointment I felt at having to take my orders from her.

'I think so,' I said. 'What's the mission?'

'Tomorrow afternoon more than a million school children are going to be marching through the streets of central London,' she replied. 'It's going to be the biggest protest rally the city has ever seen. The media are calling it the Children's Protest.'

'What are they protesting about?'

'The usual stuff,' Elliot cut in, a disdainful sneer smeared across his lips. 'Shorter lessons, less homework, easier exams – anything that will let them bunk off school and come to London to cause trouble instead.'

'That's not true,' snapped Angela, flashing Elliot an exasperated stare. 'And you know it. The government's just announced their plans to abolish school holidays and have children working all the year round. Not only that, but they're going to get pupils in school from eight in the morning until six at night – teaching us for ten hours a day! It's an outrage. The politicians say that children matter, but nobody listens to our voices. This protest is our generation's chance to make them listen.'

'So what's it got to do with the Elite?' I said, taken aback by the fiery exchange. 'It's not illegal to protest, is it?'

'Not yet,' Elliot replied, 'But the problem for us is that some people don't just want to protest. Angela – tell him what you've found out.'

A scowl still fixed to her face, Angela pulled her mobile phone out from her pocket. Sliding her finger across the screen, she pulled up a Twitter account.

'I've been monitoring social networking sites in the run up to the protest. It's standard procedure to keep our eyes open for any signs of trouble. If protestors are planning anything naughty, then we can pick up the chatter beforehand and tip off the police.'

Her finger slid across the surface of the screen as she scrolled through her tweets.

'So far most of the messages about the protest have been harmless. But I've picked up one worrying tweet. It was sent from a hijacked account on a protected network, so there's no way of telling who wrote it or who has read it. See for yourself.'

Angela handed me the phone and, glancing down at its screen, I read the message there.

3 p.m. tomorrow – zero hour. Spread the fear. Reap the whirlwind. Parliament falls. Watch for further instructions. #Children'sProtestDemolition

I looked up to see Angela's fresh-faced features creased in concern.

'The last time we picked up a message that had been sent this way was before the May Day march last year.'

The May Day march. I could remember in sickening detail the events of that terrible day eight months earlier. Thousands of people had been marching peacefully through the streets of London. Then, in an instant, everything had changed. I'd been in school when news of the explosion broke. I could remember the teacher stopping the lesson to reveal the appalling news. Then when I'd got home, I'd sat dumbfounded in front of the dreadful pictures on the TV. The thick black smoke curling up above the fleeing protestors, the blackened bodies of the injured and the dying being dragged out on stretchers. Thirty people dead, hundreds injured – all on a single summer's day.

'But that was just an accident, wasn't it?'

'We managed to cover it up to look like one,' Elliot replied. 'A fractured gas main exploding was the story we gave the papers, but the truth was much more terrible. Multiple bombs had been hidden along the route of the march. That's what the message we picked up revealed – the plans for the attack – but we didn't realise that until the first bomb exploded. We never managed to catch the attackers, but now it looks like they're about to strike again.'

Angela reached out to take her phone back from my grasp.

'We think they're planning to use the protest march as cover for an attack on Parliament,' she said. 'MI5 are ramping up the security precautions, but they need us to crack this network and find out exactly what is being planned. Rez is working on a way to hack into the hijacked Twitter account, but we need agents on the ground to track the tweets and trace who's sending them before it's too late. If we get this wrong, the lives of thousands of children could be at stake.'

Angela paused for a moment to allow the weight of her words to hit home.

'Only Elite agents are young enough to pose as protestors. Gems will be leading the undercover team,' she continued. 'I've already briefed her and Jimi about the mission, but we need another agent at the heart of the protest to triangulate the tweets as they come through. That's the only way we're going to be able to pinpoint who's behind this planned attack –'

Elliot's voice cut across hers. 'Angela will be monitoring all communications from a mobile unit on the scene. If Rez manages to hack into the hijacked account, we should be able to disrupt the attack by sending out false information. But we need your eyes on the ground to make sure that the information we send seems real. If whoever's behind this gets even a hint that we're on to them, the whole thing could blow up in our faces.'

He took a long hard look at me.

'Are you ready to take to the streets?' he asked. 'I need you to help make sure we find this maniac and his followers before they have a chance to spill any more blood.'

My mind was racing. A madman hiding in the midst of a million protestors. And who knows how many more marching in the crowds waiting for his orders. The only trail we had to follow a hijacked Twitter account. It would be like looking for a needle in a haystack.

Elliot's challenge hung in the air between us and I remembered his initial words of warning. *There's more to being an Elite agent than just hiding away in here*. If I helped prevent this attack, then I'd prove to him that I belonged in the Elite. Trying to quell the nerves coiling in the pit of my stomach, I slowly nodded my head.

'Bring it on.'

CHAPTER NINE

'I thought that when you became a spy you got to drive fast cars and play with hi-tech gadgets.'

I stood there sullenly as Elliot clipped the wireless Bluetooth headset to my ear. Inside the back of the cramped van, there was barely room for me to move. As Elliot made the final checks to my earpiece, Angela sat hunched in front of a laptop, her eyes fixed to the screen.

'You've watched too many bad movies,' Elliot muttered in reply. 'I've told you – your mobile phone has every piece of kit you need fitted as standard: 24-megapixel camera with in-built face-recognition software, GPS receiver linked to our network of spy satellites, integrated communications network, which will keep you in touch with Angela back here at the mobile control centre and Gemma and the rest of the team on the ground.'

Outside, I could hear the sound of drums getting louder as the van slowed to a crawl. As the chants of the protestors thudded through the blacked-out windows, Angela rose her voice to give me my final instructions.

'It's two thirty p.m. – thirty minutes until zero hour. We're dropping you near the front of the march. You'll be heading north on Millbank towards the Houses of Parliament. Gems is already at Parliament Square and Jimi has just crossed Westminster Bridge.'

She reached up to hand me my mobile phone. Glancing at it, I could see a new icon nestling in the corner of the home screen. I tapped my finger against this and a map of the centre of London flashed up. I could see the curve of the River Thames, the roads across Westminster Bridge, Millbank and Birdcage Walk, all converging on the Houses of Parliament.

'I built this app from scratch to map any messages that are sent from the hijacked account. By routing them through the phones of the agents on the ground, we should be able to pinpoint exactly where the tweet is being sent from. You'll be buzzed and their location will flash up on the map within seconds of the message being sent. Keep your eye on the screen and stay in contact at all times.'

The chanting was growing louder, a primal roar of protest interspersed with shrill whistles and the banging of drums. Elliot pulled my hat down over my ears, hiding the headset from view.

'Remember, keep a low profile. We don't want anyone to suspect you're working undercover. As far as that mob out there are concerned, we want them to think you're one of them.'

Turning, he grabbed hold of the door handle, ready to slide it open as the van slowed to a stop.

'There are armed response units waiting in position all around Parliament. They just need the location of the attackers to take them down. As soon as you identify a target suspect, call it in.' His voice sharpened with an urgent note of warning. 'Don't try to take them down yourself.'

As the door slid open, the thunder of the crowds outside flooded in. Elliot slapped my back as I stepped down from the van and into the side street. At the junction twenty metres ahead, I could see a massed tide of children marching in unison, their banners waving against the sky.

'Good luck.'

Elliot slid the door closed with a slam and, in reply, the van lurched backwards, accelerating as it reversed down the side street before disappearing round the corner.

I was on my own.

My mind raced with the training exercises Elliot had drilled into me back at Elite HQ. Hurrying towards the junction, I kept my mobile gripped in my right hand, waiting for the tell-tale buzz that would tell me the mission had come alive. As I neared the marching crowd, I heard the crackle of Angela's voice in my ear.

'This is Control. Status check – all agents report in. Luke, are you in position yet?'

Keeping my head down, I stepped out of the side street and into the relentless tide of teenagers marching in one direction. Above the waving banners silhouetted against the sky, I could see the Houses of Parliament, its gothic towers half hidden behind the leaves of the trees lining the road. The chorus of chants rippled through the crowd.

'We didn't vote for longer school days – hands off our holidays!'

'I'm heading north on Millbank,' I replied, trying to make myself heard over the noise of the crowd. 'Should reach Parliament in ten minutes' time.'

Next to me, a dreadlocked youth in a red Anarchy T-shirt glanced across at me.

'Sing up, bruv,' he shouted. 'Let's wake up those dodgy politicians. Just because we can't vote doesn't mean they can ignore us.'

I raised my hand in agreement as, in my ear, Jimi and Gemma's voices came through over the connection.

'This is Jimi – I'm five minutes away from Whitehall. A splinter group of protestors are trying to climb Big Ben, but the police have got them under control. I don't think they're who we're looking for. I'll keep heading towards Parliament Square and rendezvous there.'

'This is Gems – I'm in position opposite the members' entrance at the House of Commons. There are thousands of teenagers here already, but the police lines are holding firm. I'll keep monitoring all communications.'

As we marched forward, the entire street was packed from pavement to pavement. I glanced around at the smiling faces of the young protestors, their chants getting louder and more excited as we neared the Houses of Parliament. Scattered teachers and parents were marching in step with them and yellow-jacketed stewards lined the route.

The mood of the crowd seemed jubilant, no sign of any trouble brewing. Every single person joined together with one purpose – all part of something bigger than themselves. In a strange way it reminded me of how I'd started to feel since I'd joined the Elite.

Glancing down at my phone, the map of London was still clear. No messages coming through. The time at the top of my screen read 2.45 p.m. Fifteen minutes to go.

Angela's voice sounded hopefully in my ear.

'There's still no sign of any tweets from the hijacked account. They're leaving it late to make their move. Maybe it's a false alarm.'

I felt my shoulders sag in relief, not realising until that moment the tension wired through my frame. Around me, the crowd cheered as the yellow-jacketed stewards began to shepherd the march into Parliament Square. A forest of homemade signs and banners waved in celebration as they joined the crowds gathering in the shadow of Whitehall. As I followed the masses through the gates, I felt a twinge of frustration too, disappointed that my first field mission had been such a non-event.

The buzz of the mobile in my hand drilled my eyes downwards. I saw a tweet flash across the screen.

This is Red Leader. Take your positions. Automatic weapons – rapid fire. No mercy. No surrender. On my command. #Children'sProtestDemolition

I froze in fear, my heartbeat racing as the message faded and the map of London reappeared on the screen. Shaking my head, I struggled to make sense of what I saw. Where before the map had been clear, now a forest of red flashing lights lit up every location shown. It was impossible. According to this, the message had been sent from every single mobile phone in range, even my own. The attack was imminent, but from this there was no way of telling where it would come from.

Angela's voice came through on my earpiece as I started to sprint towards the Houses of Parliament, weaving my way through the crowds of protestors.

'We've got a problem,' she said.

CHAPTER TEN

'I can see there's a problem,' I gasped as I battled my way towards the looming Parliament building. Angry faces turned towards me as I elbowed a path through the crowd. 'You said this app would pinpoint exactly where this maniac is sending his orders from. Well, according to the map on my screen, he's everywhere!'

My heart thudded in my chest as I neared the front of the crowd. Straight ahead, I could see the clock tower of Big Ben reaching up into the clear blue sky. Not a hint of a cloud on the horizon, but someone in this crowd was going to bring a hard rain of terror crashing down if we didn't find them in time.

Angela's voice crackled in my ear. 'They've hacked into every mobile phone in the Parliament area,' she said. I could hear the rising note of panic in her words. 'Red Leader has turned them into zombie devices and is now controlling them remotely to pump out his orders from the hijacked Twitter account. Rez is trying to crack the hack, but if he doesn't manage it in time …'

Her voice tailed off into silence, but as I darted through the front lines of protestors, I knew what she had left unsaid. Less than ten minutes until disaster struck.

I was skirting past the north-west corner of the Palace of Westminster, a thick line of armed riot police stopping the teenage protestors from getting too close to Parliament. Homemade placards and banners waved in defiance, but the mood in the crowd was still celebratory. Their chants rang out across Parliament Square.

'The children have spoken – hear our voices. Change your minds and give us choices.'

I felt my mobile vibrate in my hand and glancing down, saw another tweet flash up on the screen.

This is Red Leader. The time is now. Are all soldiers in position? Confirm your status. #Children'sProtestDemolition

It was happening and there was nothing I could do to stop it. In desperation, I glanced back at the crowd behind me. A sea of young faces were raised in hope and expectation – the killers hidden in their midst.

The low growl of Elliot's voice came through on my earpiece.

'Abort the mission – clear the area,' he ordered. 'I need you all safe.'

Gemma's voice crackled back in reply.

'It's too late. There's no way we could get clear in time.'

With a sinking sense of despair, I stared down at the phone in my hand. With the processing power hidden inside, I could hack into the most sophisticated computer ever built, but all that was useless to me now.

Then Angela's voice buzzed in my ear again.

'There are more messages coming through in reply,' she said. 'I'm mapping them on to your screens.'

On the map, I saw three flashing blue dots appear scattered among the forest of pulsing red lights.

> This is Torch. I'm in position and awaiting your command. #Children'sProtestDemolition

> Trident here – ready for action on your command. #Children'sProtestDemolition

> This is Tornado. I'm armed and in position. Just give me the order and let's get the fireworks started. #Children'sProtestDemolition

On the screen, three locations round the Houses of Parliament shone like beacons. The terrorists had broken their cover. This was the breakthrough we needed. In my ear, I heard Elliot bark out an order.

'Send in the armed response units. Take the terrorist scum down before Red Leader has a chance to order the attack.'

I glanced down at the phone in my hand. The on-screen clock read 2.57 p.m. Three minutes until zero hour. Would the armed response teams be able to find them in time? If only there was a way I could help them.

As I stared at the phone, the realisation hit me between the eyes. If Red Leader had hacked into every mobile phone in the area to send out his orders, then I could send my own orders too. Sliding my finger across the screen, I brought up the hijacked Twitter account. The chilling trail of tweets Red Leader had already sent scrolled down the screen.

Frantically, I tapped out my message.

This is Red Leader. Hold your fire. Abort the attack and await further orders. #Children'sProtestDemolition

Pressing SEND, I prayed that it would work. Behind me, I felt the crowd suddenly surge forward. Glancing back in confusion, I saw a squad of riot officers forcing their way through the milling throng. One of the demonstrators, a heavy-set youth wearing a black combat jacket was trying to run. In his hand, I glimpsed a cold flash of steel.

The panicking lines of protestors pushed forward again, eager to get away from the trouble. Twisting my neck, I saw the riot police swarm round the youth. Slamming him to the ground, they pinned his arms behind him. One down, three to go.

I felt the phone buzz in my hand as a new tweet came through on the feed.

This is the real Red Leader. Our communications have been infiltrated. The attack is go – fire at will. #Children'sProtestDemolition

Watching the screen, I held my breath as, one by one, the flashing blue dots on the map blinked out of existence – the terrorists taken out by the armed response units. The clock read 3.00 p.m.

I heard Angela's voice crackling in my ear.

'Rez has broken the mobile-phone hijack,' she said. 'Red Leader's real location is coming through on your screens right now.'

On the map, the blizzard of blinking red lights covering the map started to fade, leaving only one behind. A pulsing spot of red light located at the entrance to the Houses of Parliament itself. The same entrance that was straight ahead of me.

I looked up in surprise. Thick lines of police stood guard at the entrance, their batons drawn in case the crowd surged forward again. Their faces were hidden behind riot helmets, automatic weapons held in holsters at their sides. At the front of the lines, I glimpsed a uniformed officer standing slightly apart. The stripes on his sleeve showed that he was in charge. He was holding a mobile phone, frantically tapping out a message with his free hand.

Immediately, the mobile phone in my own hand buzzed in warning. I glanced down to read the tweet as it appeared on my screen.

> Torch, Trident, Tornado – I repeat, our communication network has been cracked. Launch the attack now! #Children'sProtestDemolition

I looked up to see the police commander staring out into the crowd as though searching for something or someone. As I met his gaze, I saw a flash of hatred in his eyes. In an instant, I knew who he was. Red Leader – the terrorist mastermind behind this planned attack. He had been hiding in plain sight all this time.

In my ear, I heard Elliot's growl.

'Luke – you're the nearest agent to Red Leader's location. Try to establish visual contact, but make no attempt to detain him. The armed response team will be with you in one minute.'

With a sudden lurch of fear, I saw the police commander shake his head decisively, a snarl curling his lip. His hand began to reach towards the holster on his waist and the gun that was waiting there. He was ready to launch the attack alone.

'Luke – confirm my command.' Elliot's voice rose in warning. 'Do not try to take him down on your own.'

There was no time to answer – only to act. There was only one way I'd have a chance of getting close enough to stop him. Grabbing a fallen banner from the ground, I turned towards the crowd.

'Are we going to let them stop us?' I shouted as the crowd bayed in reply. 'This is our Parliament. Let's take it back!'

Turning around, I ran at full pelt towards the line of riot police blocking the entrance as the crowd surged behind me. I glimpsed the police commander's face glance up in surprise. My heart pounded in my mouth as I darted past a flailing police baton, heading straight for him.

Red Leader's fingers were still closing round his handgun as I bundled into his uniformed figure, sending him crashing against a riot shield. The line of police recoiled like a wounded animal as the protestors tried to storm the doors. Grabbing hold of the gun, I felt hands grab at my collar as we stumbled forward. The two of us locked in a deadly embrace.

As I fought to keep the weapon from his grasp, the police commander's eyes met mine. A look of pure hatred twisted his features. His elbow slammed into my stomach, driving the breath from my body with the force of the blow.

'Give me my gun,' he hissed.

Close by, I heard a policeman bark into his radio – 'Urgent back-up required' – as the mob closed round us. Dazed, I felt the gun slip from my fingers as the rogue cop wrenched it free. Dropping to my knees, I stared up in despair as, with a roar of triumph, he aimed its barrel straight at my head.

This was it. Game over.

Then, on the periphery of my vision, I glimpsed Gemma and Rez fighting their way through the chaos. The black Kevlar jackets of the armed response team swept before them like a conquering tide, their automatic rifles trained in one direction.

'Drop your weapon!' The shout rang in from all sides. 'Lie face down on the floor – now!'

Red Leader's roar of triumph was transformed into a terrifying howl of anger. He was surrounded. I watched as the gun was torn from his fingers, the armed officers forcing him to the ground.

As my heart rate slowed to a dull thunder, a hand reached out towards me. Looking up, I saw Gemma and Rez standing there.

'You're getting a bit close to the action, aren't you?' Gemma asked, a relieved smile spreading across her face.

I grinned in reply.

'What kept you?'

CHAPTER ELEVEN

'You ignored a direct order. You placed yourself and your fellow agents in the line of fire.' Elliot glared at me from across his desk. 'Give me one good reason why you should stay in the Elite.'

I stared back at him defiantly. On my return to Elite HQ, I'd expected more than a pat on the back for taking out a terrorist mastermind on my first field mission. Instead, I'd been hauled into Elliot's office and made to stand here like a naughty schoolboy while he tore me to pieces.

'Well?' said Elliot. 'I'm waiting.'

I stood there in silence, a rising tide of anger welling up inside me. If this was the thanks I got for preventing a massacre, then I was ready to walk out that door right now. I'd leave all this behind and go back to my old life as Harrison Andrews.

But could I live without the rush of adrenalin that raced through my veins as an Elite agent? I bit my tongue. Standing next to me, it was Gemma who spoke up in my defence.

'You're not being fair,' she told Elliot crossly. 'If I'd been in Luke's position, I'd have done the same. Thanks to his quick thinking we've now got a terrorist commander under interrogation. The rest of his cell are locked up in the nearest safe house. Who knows how many lives Luke saved today?'

Elliot frowned, the lines on his forehead deepening.

'I know,' he grudgingly replied. 'That's why he's still here.'

He glanced towards me again, a flicker of irritation lingering in his gaze.

'But don't think that means you can ignore my orders any time you feel like it,' he said gruffly. 'If that stunt you pulled at Parliament had gone wrong, then I'd have been zipping you into a body bag now. Remember, it's not a game – there are no second chances. You're an Elite agent – a technological whizz-kid not a junior James Bond. Leave the rough stuff to the boneheads in MI5.'

I could feel the pent-up anger that had been rising inside fade away, replaced with a sulky acceptance of Elliot's words. I remembered staring down the barrel of the gun. One squeeze of its trigger and my brains would have been splattered on the steps of Parliament. I slowly nodded my head in reply.

'I won't take a risk like that again,' I told him. The memory of Red Leader's face contorted with rage was burned into my mind. 'Why did they want to kill all those people anyway?'

Elliot shook his head.

'You don't need to know why. Here at the Elite we don't waste our time worrying about the bigger picture. We just concentrate on neutralising the danger.'

He held my gaze for a second, checking that his words had hit home. Then, finally satisfied, he turned to the open laptop on his desk.

'I've got another mission for you both,' he continued. 'An under-the-radar investigation into potentially the biggest threat to cyber-security this country has ever faced.'

He turned the laptop to face us. On its screen, I saw the instantly familiar logo that had been staring out from every billboard, TV screen and Internet pop-up ad for the past few weeks.

YourLife™

'What do you know about YourLife?' Elliot asked.

Gemma laughed. 'What *don't* we know about YourLife?' she replied with a grin. 'It's been all over the newspapers and magazines, talked about on every TV show going and the buzz about it on the Internet is unbelievable. It's not even been launched yet, but everyone is saying it's going to be the ultimate social network, the biggest the world has ever seen. It'll make Facebook, Bebo and Twitter yesterday's news.'

I nodded my head. At the moment, you couldn't turn on the TV without hearing about YourLife.

'Not just a social network,' I added. 'It's a complete digital world that will take care of you from the moment you're born until the day you die. The only place you'll ever have to go to find everything you need will be your YourLife account. They say it's going to make the Internet obsolete.'

Elliot nodded, a faint smile creeping across his face.

'I'm glad to see that you've both done your homework.'

As he tapped his finger on a wireless mouse, the YourLife logo disappeared from his laptop screen and was replaced by a photograph of a young man. Wearing a scruffy red T-shirt and jeans, he looked as though he was barely out of his teens. His blond hair was streaked by the sun and a self-confident smile played across his face.

'This is Milo Bay.' said Elliot, 'The man behind YourLife.'

I glanced across at Gemma who was leaning eagerly towards the screen, smiling as she checked out Milo Bay.

'He's nineteen years old and a multi-billionaire,' Elliot continued. 'Bay set up his first dot-com company, Milo Bay Industries, three years ago when he finished high school. It's now valued at sixty billion dollars on the New York Stock Exchange. It's the leading hi-tech business operating in the world today, with interests ranging from software and new media to online innovations and nanotechnology. You name it, whether it's a cool new app you've downloaded for your phone or the latest piece of must-have tech, the chances are Milo Bay invented it.'

'So he's rich, smart *and* good-looking,' said Gemma. I saw the smile on her face widen in delight. 'Does it get any better?'

My own face tightened in a scowl.

'I don't see what this has got to do with us,' I interrupted. 'Why are we even interested in him?'

Elliot waved me into silence.

'I'm just coming to that. Milo Bay was brought up in the United States, but he's got joint US–British citizenship through his English mother. He says that's why he's chosen the UK as the very first country to launch YourLife. Last month he signed exclusive contracts with the government to provide all their services through the YourLife platform. He's made deals with every TV channel, video-game firm, newspaper and magazine publisher in the country. Any programme you want to watch, any game you want to play, your morning newspaper or your weekly magazine – you'll find it waiting for you in YourLife.'

My jaw dropped in amazement. The hype was true. This was going to be the biggest thing to ever hit the Web.

'Under the terms of the government deal, every single UK citizen will be given a free YourLife account – even the prime minister himself.'

Elliot swept the mouse across his desk and Milo Bay's picture disappeared.

'The YourLife network is due to go live at the end of this month, but a select group of users have already signed up to trial the system and iron out any last-minute bugs. With the government contracts that are in place, we've been keeping a close eye on this trial. We need to make sure the YourLife network is everything that it's cracked up to be. But there's been a worrying development.'

He clicked the mouse again and on the laptop an online news report filled the screen. I read its headline with a growing sense of intrigue.

MYSTERY DEATHS OF CITY HIGH-FLYERS HAUNT CANARY WHARF

'In the past week, three people involved in the YourLife trial have been found dead in suspicious circumstances,' Elliot explained. 'One ran in front of a bus, another leapt from the top of the skyscraper where they worked, while the last drowned in the bath at home. The initial police investigations suggest suicide, but nobody can understand why. They all had everything to live for – top jobs, money in the bank, happy relationships. No reason to end it all. The one thing that we've found is that they were all logged on to the YourLife network minutes before their death.'

'You think there's a connection?' Gemma asked. The smile had now faded from her face.

'I don't know,' Elliot replied grimly. 'That's what I want you to find out.'

He moved the mouse across the desk again and clicked on an icon at the top right of the screen. An image of a sleek skyscraper, a high-rise arrow of glass and steel spiking the crowded London skyline, zoomed into focus.

'This is Milo Bay Industries' UK headquarters. The company is based in the heart of London's Canary Wharf. Rez and Jimi have been trying to hack into the mainframe computer there to uncover the secrets of the YourLife network, but they've had no success so far. Every attempt that the twins have made to crack the system has been shut down before they've even got past the first firewall.' Elliot ran his fingers through his closely cropped hair in frustration. 'Milo Bay has designed a security system more sophisticated than anything we even use here at Elite HQ. There's no way of accessing the YourLife mainframe from the outside. That's why we need you to go in.'

My pulse quickened. A racing drumbeat of adrenalin pumped through my veins at the thought of my next mission. The chance to pit my cyber-skills against the big shot Milo Bay. I grinned. The multi-billionaire nerd wouldn't know what hit him.

'Just tell me when you want me to go,' I said.

Elliot shook his head.

'No, Luke, you're staying here to run the remote surveillance side of the mission. You've not got enough experience to take on this kind of undercover work alone. It's Gemma who's going in.'

CHAPTER TWELVE

'This is Gems to Control. I'm inside Milo Bay Industries and have activated all data feeds. Can you confirm that you're receiving these?'

From my seat in the hub at Elite HQ, I could see Gemma staring back at me from the laptop screen. Her usual hoodie and combats combo had been replaced by a smartly tailored trouser suit. She was standing in front of a washbasin mirror, her immaculate reflection looking older than her sixteen years. I breathed out in a silent sigh. The nano-camera in her contact lens was working fine from where I was sitting.

'Luke – do you read me?'

The snap of Gemma's voice in my earpiece brought my focus back to the readings on screen.

'We've got live visual,' I replied, speaking softly into my headset. 'Audio is also on stream. Everything that you see and hear is coming right back to us at base.' I squinted at the final greyed-out bar in the data feed at the bottom of the screen. 'There's something blocking your Wi-Fi scanner, though. I'm not getting any readings from the Milo Bay Industries intranet. You're going to need to log on to it directly. It's the only way we'll be able to hack into the YourLife mainframe computer.'

On the screen, I saw Gemma's reflection quickly nod her head.

'I'll try,' she replied, 'but I won't be able to do it yet. They've told me that all new staff first have to undergo a training session before they can start work. I've only managed to sneak out now by pretending that I needed the toilet.'

There was a squeaking noise off screen, like a door being opened. Gemma quickly turned on the taps above the sink before glancing up in the direction of the sound. Through her eyes, I saw a young woman peering round the door frame. Her Milo Bay Industries security pass hung from a lanyard round her neck. I zoomed in on the screen to read the name written there: Sophie Wilkinson – Recruitment Administrator. She looked down at the folder in her hand, before glancing up at Gemma impatiently.

'If I could just hurry you along, Emma,' she sighed. 'The induction training is scheduled to start now and you are keeping the others waiting.'

Gemma nodded. Turning away from the sink, she thrust her hands into a dryer.

'I'll be right there,' she called out over its asthmatic drone. Under her breath she added, 'As soon as I get online, make sure Rez and Jimi are ready to crack the intranet. We need to find out what secrets are hidden in the YourLife system.'

As the noise of the dryer died away, I watched as Gemma followed Sophie out through the door and back into the lobby of Milo Bay Industries. An air-conditioned hum buzzed through the laptop speakers, the mobile receiver implanted in Gemma's tooth so sensitive that it picked up the slightest of sounds. As she glanced up, I saw the sheer pillars of glass and steel supporting the sweeping arches of the lobby ceiling. Above these, I caught fleeting glimpses of the hectic, bustling floors spiralling up inside the skyscraper.

Sophie escorted Gemma towards the lifts where a group of five other young men and women stood waiting. Pulling a handful of security passes from her folder, Sophie handed these to each of them in turn.

'These are temporary security passes,' she explained. 'Your photo-cards will be waiting for you at reception when you finish work tonight.'

She pressed the call button and the lift doors glided smoothly open. As Sophie ushered the new recruits inside, I saw Gemma's face reflected in the glass.

'I'm taking you up to Conference Room One for your training,' Sophie continued. 'After that, you'll each be assigned to your project teams.'

As the lift doors glided shut on screen, I felt a heavy hand rest on my shoulder. Glancing up, I saw Elliot standing there. His face was set in its usual stern line.

'What's the progress report?' he snapped. 'Are we any closer to getting inside the YourLife system?'

I shook my head.

'We still can't access the system remotely. Gemma's Wi-Fi scanner is being blocked by something inside Milo Bay Industries. We're going to try to bypass it by piggybacking our way in through the company intranet. But we've got to wait for Gemma to get in front of a computer.'

'Keep me updated,' said Elliot. 'As soon as we get inside the YourLife system, I want a full spectrum analysis run on the central server. If there's anything strange hidden away in there, I want to know about it. We're running out of time.'

'What do you mean?' I asked, thrown by the sudden urgency of Elliot's command. 'The YourLife network's not going live for another two weeks.'

Elliot's forehead furrowed in a frown.

'Milo Bay just made an announcement by satellite to every TV station in the country,' he growled in reply. 'He's bringing the launch date for YourLife network forward to the end of this week. We've got less than two days to find out what's inside. If YourLife is behind those deaths, then I need to find out how they're doing it so we can shut it down.'

Turning away, Elliot walked round the central hub to where Rez and Jimi were sitting. The brothers were hunched over twin laptop screens, working flat out to perfect the program they were building to crack open the YourLife network. Elliot rested his hands on their shoulders as their fingers raced across the keyboards.

I glanced back at my laptop.

'Did you get all that?' I whispered into my headset.

On the screen, I saw Gemma nod her head once in reply.

The lift doors opened again. As they filed out, Sophie led Gemma and the rest of the new recruits down a long corridor. Stopping at the final door on her left, marked Conference Room 1, she pushed it open and gestured for them to step inside.

At the front of the conference room, a giant video screen displayed the YourLife logo. Standing in front of this was a twenty-something man wearing a blue open-necked shirt. Next to him, his trainers resting on the large conference table that filled half the room, sat a blond-haired youth. He was staring down at the computer in his palm, but as he glanced up, I heard Gemma's low gasp of recognition.

It was Milo Bay.

CHAPTER THIRTEEN

As the new recruits settled into the empty chairs around the conference table, the man in the blue shirt began to speak.

'On behalf of Milo Bay Industries, I'd like to welcome you all on board. We only recruit the brightest of minds, so take heart in the fact that you're sitting round this table today. Now, before we get started with your training, I have the unexpected honour of introducing you to the man behind YourLife – my boss and now yours – Mr Milo Bay himself.'

A murmur of excitement spread around the room as the blond youth levered his trainers off the table and rose to his feet.

'Thanks for that, Ben,' he said, nodding his head in acknowledgement as the other man returned to his seat. 'But go easy on the "boss" thing – in the end, we're all working on this project together, right?'

Staring at the screen, I scowled as Milo Bay's transatlantic drawl crackled in my ear. *All working on this together.* That was easy for him to say with his billions in the bank. I slowly shook my head in disbelief. Was he for real? Something about his laidback manner grated on my nerves.

'Well, guys,' Milo continued, looking out at the faces round the conference table, 'I don't usually welcome every single new recruit to my company in person. With 200,000 employees in over a hundred different countries, it'd keep me kind of busy.'

A wave of nervous laughter rippled around the room.

'But as I was passing by, I just wanted to let you know that you're joining us on the eve of a groundbreaking day. The launch of the YourLife network across the United Kingdom. Now I'm sure you've all heard the buzz about this project …'

Milo tapped the screen of his hand-held computer. On the wall behind him, the video screen flickered into life: an avalanche of headlines filling the screen.

IS THIS MULTI-BILLIONAIRE MILO BAY'S BEST IDEA YET?

THE HOTTEST NEW SOCIAL NETWORK TO HIT THE BLOCK

THE ONLY THING YOU NEED IN YOUR LIFE – YOURLIFE!

With a second tap of his finger, Milo froze the flood of hype and the YourLife logo filled the screen again.

'Now these headlines only tell half the story. We all know what we want from a social network – to stay in touch with our friends, organise our lives, connect to the things that matter to us. That's what every social network from MySpace to Facebook has promised us, but YourLife is different. YourLife gives you what you really need.'

Looking out at each of the new recruits in turn, Milo's blue eyes glinted with a hungry gleam.

'Imagine a world where your computer knows exactly what you want before you even realise it yourself. Where from the moment you wake up to the second you go to sleep, you are connected to a network that tells you everything you need to know. This is what YourLife will give you.'

Milo lifted his hand-held computer in front of his face. The camera lens in its top left corner glinted red. Behind him, the faces of the new recruits around the table were displayed on the screen. The YourLife interface – icons, menus, applications and updates – was laid over the top of the image.

'When you connect to YourLife,' Milo continued, 'the real world and the digital world become one.' He moved the camera lens so that it focused on each of the recruit's faces in turn. As he did so, information about each person cascaded across the screen – their CV, web profiles, tweets – the YourLife interface constantly updating. 'The YourLife network gives you instant access to a wealth of information. Every new person you meet won't be a stranger – you'll be able to see, at a glance, the things you have in common, the friends that you share.'

He dragged his finger across the screen of his computer, moving a snapped picture of each recruit's face to a new drop-down menu.

'You'll be able to add them to your buddy list, your business contacts or even just delete them from your screen.'

His eyes narrowed as he dragged Gemma's snapshot to the red cross of the delete icon. His gaze flicked for a second to her face, but then Milo turned his attention back to the screen behind him.

'And that's just the start,' he continued smoothly. 'It's not just the people you meet that you can connect with. Everywhere that you go, everything that you see – the YourLife network will connect you to the information you need.'

On the screen, a video showed a teenage boy and girl walking hand in hand down a busy high street. Then the camera angle switched to show the same street through their eyes. The YourLife interface added a digital layer to the scene, filling the street with glittering icons. As the icon in front of each shop-front was clicked, a cascading waterfall of information ran down the screen. Record shops streaming music, video links to the latest fashion collections, video-game stores offering demo downloads – the real world as seen through a computer screen.

I shook my head in wonder as I stared at the image on my own laptop. This was going to change everything. The technology YourLife was using was cutting edge. It was more advanced even than some of the hi-tech tools the Elite used. Milo Bay must have invested billions in developing this. And he was giving it away for free. What was in it for him?

'YourLife will give you freedom,' Milo bragged. 'Freedom from boredom. Freedom from ignorance. Everything and everyone will be connected.'

All round the table, the new recruits broke into spontaneous applause. In my earpiece I heard the soft murmur of Gemma's voice as her gaze stayed fixed on Milo Bay. 'He should be working for us.'

I felt a pang of jealousy as I saw Milo turn towards Blue-shirt Ben who was now rising from his seat.

'I'll leave you now in Ben's capable hands to start your training,' Milo said as he pocketed his mini-computer. 'I wish you all the best of luck.'

Stepping out from behind the long conference table, Milo headed for the door. As Gemma's gaze followed him out of the room, he cast a wary glance back at her. His lips creased in a half smile as their eyes met. Then the door closed behind him.

Walking round the table, Ben presented each of them with their own hand-held computer. Gemma looked down at the Milo Bay Industries logo edged in silver along the sleek black case.

'These are your computers,' Ben explained. 'As you'll see, we've already set each of you up with your own YourLife account. This is the gateway to your training program. Once you log on, you'll see for yourself the power of the YourLife network. Try it out.'

Turning the computer over in her hand, Gemma tapped her finger against the YourLife logo in the middle of the screen. All round her, the other new recruits were doing the same. On her computer screen, the YourLife interface swam into view.

Quickly, Gemma ran her finger down the list of menu options. Finding the icon for the Milo Bay Industries intranet, she tapped her finger against it twice.

'We're in,' she breathed.

Back at Elite HQ, my laptop came alive with a mirror image of the Milo Bay Industries intranet. Gemma had done it; she'd unlocked the back door. Now it was up to Rez and Jimi to use the intranet to break in to the YourLife system and find out exactly how it worked.

I swivelled on my chair to face them across the hub.

'Rez, Jimi,' I called out. The twins glanced up immediately. 'Gemma's patched us into their intranet. It's all systems go. We need to get inside the YourLife servers.'

Devilish smiles creased the brothers' faces as they cracked their knuckles in unison. 'We're on it.'

Turning back to my laptop, I saw that Gemma's gaze was fixed on Ben. He was standing at the head of the conference-room table, while behind him the YourLife interface filled the video screen.

'This is YourLife,' he explained. 'Everything you ever need will be delivered to you through this screen. On the left-hand side, you'll see your bulletin board. This will channel every message you need to read. Let's give it a try.'

Ben pulled out his own mini-computer and tapped out a message on its screen. Instantly, every device around the table pinged in reply and Gemma glanced down to read the message as it appeared on her bulletin board.

Watching on my laptop, the screen suddenly flickered as Gemma's eyes swam out of focus. A fuzzy image blinked in and out of existence across the screen. I spoke softly into my headset.

'Gemma, it looks like we've got a malfunction. I think the nano-camera in your contact lens is on the fritz.'

There was no reply.

'Gemma, do you read me?' I asked, an uneasy feeling starting to knot in my stomach.

From the laptop speakers, I heard a dull thumping sound. The blurred image on the screen shimmered into focus for a second. I had to crane my neck to see the picture, the image twisted at a ninety-degree angle.

I glimpsed the new recruits slumped unconscious, their faces pressed against the conference-room table. Then the screen turned black.

CHAPTER FOURTEEN

With my cap pulled low over my eyes, I pushed the floor cleaner along the corridor of Milo Bay Industries. Outside, the dull grey edges of a wintry morning were staining the sky. Soon these corridors would be bustling again with busy employees, racing to finish work on the YourLife network ready for its launch. I just hoped that I could find Gemma among them.

Ever since the screen on my laptop had faded to black nearly twenty hours earlier, our connection to Gemma had been lost. We'd had no word from her since then. No way of knowing if she was dead or alive. Every attempt we had made to hack into the skyscraper's network of CCTV cameras to find out what was happening had been locked out. Rez and Jimi had only just managed to keep our connection to the YourLife mainframe computer.

Finally, Elliot had been forced to call in MI5 to ask for their help. They'd sent in a couple of their best agents to locate and retrieve Gemma. For a long night we'd waited for any news. Then, before dawn broke, the bodies of both agents had been fished out of the River Thames. The police on the scene had called it in as a double suicide. But there was still no sign of Gemma.

Back at Elite HQ, Elliot had called me into his office. Slumped behind his desk, his face was as grey as the dawn. As he spoke, Elliot rubbed the shadow of stubble on his face in frustration.

'It's a disaster. Two MI5 operatives dead, Gems still missing in action and the YourLife network goes live in less than five hours. For the last hour, I've been speaking to the prime minister asking for authorisation to shut YourLife down. He says that without any direct evidence linking Milo Bay Industries to illegal activity the launch must go ahead.' He shook his head, his features hardening into a grim mask of determination. 'We're on our own.'

I swallowed down the bitter taste of guilt rising in my throat. My job on this mission had been to be Gemma's lifeline – to keep her in contact with Elite HQ at all times. I'd let her down.

'So what are we going to do?' I asked.

'Rez and Jimi are working flat out to make sense of the YourLife systems,' Elliot replied. 'They say that the computer code behind the network is the most sophisticated they've ever seen. We need them to find out exactly what Milo Bay has built here and what he has to hide. But we're running out of time.'

Looking up, Elliot fixed me with an unblinking stare. His haggard face was creased into a craggy frown. 'There's only one option left,' he said. 'I want you to infiltrate Milo Bay Industries.'

I stared back at him astounded. After everything he'd said the last time I'd gone undercover, he now wanted me to go in there alone. Seeing my stunned reaction, he slowly nodded his head.

'You're right. If I could send anyone else in there apart from you, I would. You're undisciplined, impulsive – you haven't even finished your Elite training yet. But you were Gemma's liaison from the second she stepped into that skyscraper to the moment we lost contact with her. That means you know the set-up at Milo Bay Industries better than anyone else on the team. I want you to get in there, find Gemma and stop the launch of the YourLife network by any means possible.'

I nodded my head. This was my chance to put things right. I wouldn't let Gemma down this time. There was only one question left to ask.

'How am I going to get in there?'

That was when Elliot pulled out the set of cleaner's overalls.

As I reached the end of the corridor, I switched off the floor cleaner, sighing with relief as its drone faded away. I had to hand it to Elliot though, dressed like this nobody had even given me a second glance. They'd even covered my chin in fake stubble back at base to make me look old enough to begin work as an Environment Improvement Operative.

I had arrived at Milo Bay Industries before the start of the working day, joining the rest of the cleaners as we silently entered the building through raised metal shutters. Once inside, we pulled on our overalls and lined up to be armed with an array of mops, brushes and floor cleaners. The skyscraper's hundred floors rose above us, waiting to be cleaned.

First of all, I'd headed for the last place I'd seen Gemma alive – Conference Room 1. When I got there, the room was empty. As I walked round the large table, I couldn't shake the blurred image from my mind: every single one of Milo Bay Industries' new recruits slumped unconscious. What had happened to them? Back at Elite HQ, they'd come up with countless theories – some kind of nerve gas was the latest favourite – but I needed to find out the truth.

Outside, the corridor was deserted. As I pushed the floor cleaner towards the lifts, my brain ran through the sequence of events for the thousandth time. Milo Bay's slick presentation, the sleek mini-computers handed round the table, Gemma logging on to her YourLife account for the very first time. YourLife. That was at the heart of this mystery. If only Rez and Jimi could hurry up and untangle its code to find out how.

Reaching the lift, I scanned the list of floors. I quickly located the YourLife division – their offices taking up the entire forty-third floor. I pushed the call button for the lift and, almost instantly, the doors pinged open. As I stepped inside, I felt the buzz of the mobile receiver implanted in my tooth.

'Luke,' Elliot's voice crackled directly into my brain. 'Give me an update on your progress.'

I winced. My jaw still ached from where the dental surgeon had implanted the device.

'Apart from the cleaners and security guards, the offices seem deserted,' I replied. 'No sign of Gems.'

Turning to the control panel, I pressed the button marked 43 and the lift doors began to slide shut.

'I'm heading for the YourLife division now. Maybe I'll find some answers there.'

The lift slowly began to climb as Elliot's voice buzzed in my brain in reply.

'Rez and Jimi have made a breakthrough with their analysis of the YourLife computer servers. I'm patching Jimi in so he can explain it himself.'

The excited tones of Jimi's voice came through over the connection.

'Luke, you wouldn't believe what we're finding here. The computer code they've used to program the YourLife network is like nothing I've ever seen before. It's as though we're looking inside a computerised mind. Inside the code, there are what seem to be brainwaves pulsing backwards and forwards. They're streaming into the mainframe computer from every trial YourLife users' account.'

'Wait a second,' I replied, trying to keep up with Jimi's explanation. 'What are you trying to say? That the YourLife network can read your mind?'

'Not just read it,' said Jimi. 'Theoretically, this computer code could be used to control brainwaves too. The YourLife network could be used to program your behaviour.'

The lift hummed to a stop. Floor 43.

'Luke, you need to –'

Jimi's voice started to break up, the connection suddenly dissolving in a burst of static. Then the line went dead.

As the lift doors slid back to reveal the secrets of the forty-third floor, my eyes widened in surprise. It was the same open-plan office I had seen on every floor of the skyscraper so far. Endless rows of cubicles with state-of-the-art computers gracing every desk. But every single desk here was occupied: hundreds of employees peering intently at their monitors with unblinking stares. The only sound I could hear was the constant clicking of their fingers across computer keyboards.

A digital display on the wall read 1:47. As I watched, the last digit flipped from a seven to a six. 1:46. It was counting down. Less than two hours to go before the YourLife network went live across the UK. I was running out of time.

Warily, I stepped out of the lift. I immediately saw a security guard in front of a coffee machine, some twenty metres away on my right. The machine's throaty gurgle masked the soft ping of the lift doors as they closed behind me. Keeping low, I scuttled forward, heading for the shelter of the nearest empty cubicle.

Oblivious, the security guard took a noisy slurp from his coffee. Then he turned and headed towards the lift. From my hiding place, I watched as he pressed the call button and, as the lift doors slid open in reply, stepped inside. Then the doors closed and the lift began to descend.

The coast was clear. Now I had to find Gemma.

Rising to my feet, I scanned the vast workspace. All around me I could see young men and women hunched in front of monitors. Every single face was lit by a digital glow. I started to walk the aisles, peering over every cubicle wall as I searched for Gems. Not one person looked up as I passed; their dead eyes fixed to their screens.

Then I saw her. Blonde bobbed hair clipped back from her face, Gemma sat in front of a computer. Her blue eyes flicked back and forth across its screen as her fingers raced across the keyboard. I let out a grateful sigh of relief. She was alive.

Stepping round the cubicle, I tapped her lightly on the shoulder.

'Gemma.'

Dragging her gaze away from the screen, she glanced up at me with unblinking eyes.

'What happened?' I asked. 'You've been out of contact for over twenty hours. We thought you'd been taken prisoner – maybe even killed.'

She stared back at me quizzically.

'Who are you?'

CHAPTER FIFTEEN

'What do you mean? It's me – Luke.'

Gemma had already turned back to her screen. Without a second glance at me, her fingers started tapping away at the keyboard again.

I stared at her confused. Why was she acting like she didn't even know me? Was she trying to save me from blowing my cover? I glanced around, searching for any sign of hidden CCTV cameras or people listening in. There was nothing. In the adjoining cubicles, the workers just sat staring straight ahead at their own screens. Nobody had even noticed I was there.

I turned back to Gemma. On her monitor, complex lines of computer code scrolled down the screen as her fingers danced across the keyboard.

'What are you doing?' I asked her.

'Preparing the YourLife network for launch,' she replied, keeping her eyes fixed to the screen. 'The project must succeed.'

Gemma's voice sounded strained, almost as though she was speaking the words against her will.

I grabbed hold of her hand, trying to wrench Gemma's attention away from the screen.

'Gems – this isn't you. That's not what you're here for.'

She glared up at me.

'That's why we're all here. Now leave me in peace,' she hissed. Her eyes flicked over my overalls. 'Haven't you got some floors to clean?'

I stepped back in horror. This wasn't an act. She didn't know who I was or what we had been sent here to do. What had they done to her?

Gemma turned back to face the screen, her fingers already racing across the keyboard again. What was I supposed to do now? I thought that when I found Gemma, we'd be able to work together to stop Milo Bay from launching the YourLife network. But here she was, feverishly working to make it succeed. I needed help.

Turning away, I opened my mouth and tapped my back tooth with my finger. The mobile receiver implanted there buzzed into life.

'Luke to Control – I've found Gems, but we've got a problem.'

In reply, a dull roar of static filled my brain. I tapped my tooth again, desperately trying to open the communication link to Elite HQ. The connection stayed down. There must be something blocking it. I was on my own.

I tried to remember what Jimi had told me before I lost contact with him back at base. Something about the code used to program the YourLife network ... *Brainwaves pulsing backwards and forwards ... streaming into the mainframe computer from every trial YourLife user's account.* In my mind's eye, I saw the new recruits slumped around the conference table. I remembered the message pinging into their YourLife accounts moments before Gemma slipped into unconsciousness.

That was it! Jimi had said that the YourLife network could be used to read minds and control them too. That must be why Gemma was acting so strangely now. Mind control.

The truth dawning, I looked around the open-plan office again. The countless rows of workers, heads bent to their tasks. Nobody talking or even pausing for a moment. A silent army of brainwashed drones under YourLife's command.

There had to be some way I could break the program. I glanced back at Gemma. Her unblinking stare was still fixed to the computer screen. No chance of any help there. However, in the next row, I glimpsed an empty cubicle, the computer sitting there left unattended. A way inside the YourLife system.

Quickly, I made my way to the empty cubicle. Sliding into the chair, I booted up the computer. In an instant, the YourLife login page appeared on the screen. Two blank boxes asked for my username and password. Just one problem – I didn't have a YourLife account – but that was nothing a little social engineering couldn't fix.

I reached into the pocket of my overalls and pulled out my key ring. Instead of a bunch of keys that would unlock doors, I had something much more useful. An array of USB flash drives and memory sticks hung from the key ring. On these were programs that could crack passwords, bypass security systems, unlock any computer. I even had the Apocalypse Worm trapped on a crimson-red memory stick: a souvenir of my first success as an Elite agent.

Selecting a black USB key, I inserted it into the computer's drive. Then typing out a single command, I activated the password-cracking program lurking in its files. The screen filled with thousands of usernames, each one gradually revealing its password alongside as the program worked its magic. I searched through the list for the name of Gemma's undercover identity: Emma Smith. Next to her username, I saw her password appear on the screen – servus953.

Closing the window, I logged on to the YourLife network. Instantly, its familiar interface filled the screen, Gemma's YourLife profile open for me to see. I could see the messages that filled her bulletin board – a series of orders from Milo Bay Industries.

Everything that she did was being dictated by YourLife.

There was no time to work out how to stop these orders. The Elite needed her back working for us now. There was only one thing I could do. Delete the account.

I moved the mouse along the menu bar. Finding the account-settings menu, I clicked on the option to delete the account. Nothing happened. I clicked again and then a new message appeared on the screen.

Unauthorised action selected. Request denied.

My head sank into my hands. How could I have been so dumb? Of course, Milo Bay wouldn't build a brainwashing machine like this and then leave the key to escape it on the front page. I racked my brain. There must be a way to bypass the system.

Every system had one. A trap door that allowed the person running the network to make any changes required. It could be a single word – a code that would unlock the system. If only I could find it. I ran every hack that I knew, but whatever key I pressed or command I typed to try to wipe the account, the screen spat out the same reply.

Unauthorised action selected. Request denied.

Then it hit me. With quicksilver fingers, I brought up the list of usernames again. I scrolled down it until I found the name I was looking for: Milo Bay. There was his password, five letters long: PAREO.

With a flicker of hope still burning, I typed in the word and clicked on the deactivate button again. On the screen, the YourLife interface froze before turning to grey. A ghost image of Gemma's profile hung there. Then a message flashed up on the screen:

Account deleting.

Beneath this, a progress bar crept steadily forward. With bated breath, I watched as it neared completion. Then the screen slowly turned to white before being replaced by a second message.

YourLife has ended.

Jubilant, I turned to look at Gemma. She was frozen, her eyes gazing into the distance in a thousand-yard stare. A thin line of blood trickled from her nose.

Racing to her side, I grabbed hold of Gemma before she slumped over the desk. I cradled her head in my hands.

'Gemma! Are you OK?'

She stared up at me through blinking eyes.

'Luke – is that you?'

I nodded my head.

'Come on, we've got to get out of here.'

I helped Gemma up from her chair. She winced as she took a step forward.

'My legs are numb,' she groaned. 'I must have been sitting there for hours.'

Hooking a supporting arm around her shoulders, we started to hobble towards the lift doors. In their cubicles on either side of the aisle, the office workers stayed hunched in front of their computers. Not a single person looked up as we passed.

'It was like I was dreaming,' said Gemma, her face creased into a puzzled frown. 'I forgot I was undercover. I thought I really was Emma Smith. There was something telling me exactly what I had to do. I was powerless to resist.'

'That was the YourLife network,' I told her. 'It was inside your mind. We've got to stop them before they launch it across the country. Otherwise, every single person in Britain will be under their control.'

We had almost reached the coffee machine now. Only another twenty metres to go before we made it to the safety of the lift.

'There must be a way we can take out the entire YourLife network,' I said. 'If we can just find a weakness somewhere in the system.'

'I don't think so.'

The confident drawl of a voice from directly behind us stopped me in my tracks. Glancing back, I saw Milo Bay advancing towards us. He was tapping at the screen of his hand-held computer.

'You see, I built the YourLife system myself,' he continued. 'The security systems I designed protect the entire network from any act of sabotage or cyber-attack. Its computer servers are secured in a bunker beneath this skyscraper, which can withstand a direct nuclear strike.' With a taunting stare, Milo met my gaze and smiled. 'There are no weaknesses.'

The cruel expression on his face reminded me of an overgrown child toying with a captured insect.

'Now what are we going to do with you both?'

CHAPTER SIXTEEN

Milo walked slowly towards us. His every step was like a caged panther's, full of menace. He was on his own, but something in his twisted smile told me that he held all the cards.

'How did you find us?' I asked, desperately playing for time as we backed away.

'YourLife tells me everything that I need to know,' Milo replied. 'Did you really think you could use my password without my noticing? Thanks for the heads-up, though. It's good to get a reminder to change password from time to time. Helps to keep things secure.'

I tried not to let the disappointment show on my face. With his password changed, the trap door I'd found that led inside the YourLife system was locked for good.

Our shuffling retreat was brought to a sudden halt. The rattle of cups told me we were backed up against the coffee machine. I glanced across at Gems. Her green eyes blazed angrily as she jabbed her finger at Milo.

'What do you think you're playing at? That program of yours brainwashed me.'

'I know.' Milo smiled proudly. 'Cool, isn't it?'

Looking at his smug grin, an idea sparked in my mind.

Milo Bay might be a multi-billionaire, but I could tell there was one thing bigger than his bank account – his ego. Maybe that would give us the chance to find out exactly what we were dealing with here.

'So how does it work then?' I asked. 'You just plug us into the YourLife network and we're under your control?'

'Oh yeah, that's right,' Milo laughed in reply. 'I forgot. This is the part where I explain how clever I've been and reveal all my plans.'

The spark of cunning in my eyes faded as quickly as it had arrived.

'Not that it matters,' Milo continued. He slid his finger across the screen of his computer. 'The two of you aren't really in a position to do anything about it now. In fact, it would be quite satisfying to explain the secret of YourLife to someone who might even understand it.' He lifted his computer to frame us in its camera lens and then stared at the screen. 'You are both Elite agents after all.'

Gemma and I exchanged an anxious glance. Our cover was blown.

'I made the breakthrough just over a year ago. The US military had given me a three-billion-dollar contract to research the development of computers that could directly link to their soldiers' brains. They wanted to transmit the information soldiers needed for their missions straight into their minds. The idea was that soldiers could then use the same data link to transmit what they saw, what they heard, even what they were thinking, back to base during the mission. A hi-tech network to cut through the fog of war.'

Milo came to a halt, standing only a few metres away. His finger idly tapped at the screen of his computer as he carried on speaking.

'Using cutting-edge brain scanners, I began to decode the language of the human mind. Brainwaves pulsing through networks of neurons, gigabytes of data electrically transmitted through the hard-wiring of our minds. It was just a matter of converting it all into a computer code. As I worked, I realised how pathetic the army's ambitions for the technology I was building really were. Why just try to read brainwaves when you could control them? That's when I decided to create YourLife: a neuro-cybernetic network that could program the behaviour of every single person who is connected to it.'

Milo smiled indulgently as he watched the first glimmer of understanding flicker across my face.

'That's right. When you log on to the YourLife network, you're giving control of your life to me. I can make you buy anything that I want you to, go anywhere that I send you, do anything that I ask – even kill.'

Gemma gasped.

'Those people who were trialling YourLife,' she said. 'The man who ran in front of a bus, the person who jumped from the skyscraper, the woman who drowned in her own bath. You murdered them!'

Milo shook his head.

'I just sent the orders over the YourLife network. I needed to see how far its power over a user's mind really went.' An impish grin split his face. 'All the way, it seems.'

Above his head, the digital display on the wall read 1:30. Only one and a half hours before the YourLife network went live across the UK. Even though my worst fears had been growing from the moment Milo had started speaking, my mind still reeled in horror at the revelation. The entire population could be transformed into killers under Milo Bay's command.

'I decided to launch YourLife in the United Kingdom first,' Milo continued. 'Give me a chance to iron any bugs out of the system before taking it worldwide.' He ran his fingers through his sun-streaked hair, a smart-alec sneer creasing his face. 'Did the Elite really think you could stop me?'

Gemma glared back at him defiantly.

'Yes – and we will.'

Milo laughed. Glancing down, he tapped at the screen of his computer.

'I admire your single-minded resolve,' he smiled. 'But are you really sure? You see, the central servers keep a back-up of every YourLife profile. It's simply just a matter of restoring your account.' He looked up from the screen. 'There.'

With a sudden sense of dread, I glanced across at Gemma. Her face was frozen into a frown.

'Gems,' I murmured.

She ignored me, her unblinking eyes staring vacantly ahead.

The chilling realisation slowly dawned. YourLife had control of her mind again.

'Do you still think you can stop me?' Milo crowed. He tapped his computer screen once more. Across the vast open-plan office, every single worker rose to their feet. Stepping out from their cubicles, they turned towards Milo Bay. A hundred pairs of eyes stared blankly ahead as if awaiting his command. 'You and whose army?'

I cast a despairing glance towards the lift, still only twenty metres away. It might as well have been twenty miles. Between there and here, dozens of silent soldiers stood waiting by their desks. Ready to kill if that's what YourLife ordered them to do. There was no way I could fight my way past them.

Milo's grin widened. His fingers hovered above the mini-computer cradled in his left hand. If only I could get away before he had a chance to send his order.

With a trickle of sweat beading my forehead, I carefully reached out for the work surface behind me. Hidden by Gemma's frozen figure, my fingers scrabbled among the debris littered around the coffee machine. If I could just find something that could distract him for long enough ...

My hand brushed against a glass jar sitting at the base of the coffee machine. Straining my fingers, I reached for its handle, but it was just out of reach. There was only one way I could lift it. I closed my hand round the glass jug, feeling its heat burning my fingers. As I tried to lever it from the machine, I saw Milo moving his finger towards the touch screen again. I needed more time.

'Why are you doing this?' I asked, fighting to keep the pain from my voice. 'You're already a multi-billionaire – you've got everything you could possibly want.'

Milo glanced up, his finger still poised above the screen.

'Is that what you think?' He laughed hollowly. 'Well, I've got news for you, buddy – I'm bored. All that money, it means nothing without power – real power. That's what I want.' His eyes glittered with a steely determination. 'The world is ruled by fools and liars. I could do a much better job. That's why I built the YourLife network. When the whole world is connected, I'll be in charge. Presidents, prime ministers, dictators and kings – they'll all take their orders from me.'

Milo spread his arms wide, a crazed grin of triumph slashed across his face.

'The geek shall inherit the earth!'

I finally prised the jug free with a click. Boiling hot coffee slopped over the side, scalding my already stinging fingers. Mistakenly taking my wince of pain for concern, Milo shook his head.

'Don't worry. With the power of the YourLife network controlling their minds, everyone will think they're living in paradise.' With a grin, he glanced down at the computer in his hand. 'Now it's time we got you connected too.'

This was it – my only chance. Pushing Gemma clear, I hurled the coffee pot straight at Milo Bay. His smug grin instantly turned to a grimace. With a sudden crack of impact, the glass jug smacked the computer out of his hand. As the pot shattered, shards flying in every direction, the device skittered across the floor.

Screaming with pain, Milo dropped to his knees. Watching in silence, the countless rows of workers stood motionless, still frozen and awaiting his command. I turned and ran for the lift.

I pounded on the call button. The lift doors slowly slid open and I scrambled inside. Glancing back, I saw Milo scrabbling to reach his computer. His hand closed round it and his fingers danced across its screen as he typed out his order.

'Kill him!' he roared.

As one, the massed ranks of office workers turned to face me. Their blank stares now glittered with malice. They began to march towards the lift, grabbing lamps, paper knives and hard drives from their desks – anything they could use as a weapon.

I hammered on the control panel. As the doors slid together with agonising slowness, I glimpsed Gemma at the front of the mob. She was staring straight at me with murder in her eyes. For a second, our eyes met and then the lift doors snapped shut.

CHAPTER SEVENTEEN

As the lift slowly climbed to the sound of people hammering on the doors below, I racked my brain for a way out of this nightmare. It was worse than we had feared. Milo Bay was going to use the YourLife network to take over the world.

With Gems brainwashed, I desperately needed some back-up to help me stop him. Tapping my back tooth, I tried again to open the comms link to Elite HQ. The mobile receiver buzzed into life, but only a dull roar of static came through on the line. I clenched my fists in frustration. Something was still jamming the connection.

I glanced at the lift's control panel. The numbers on the buttons reached up to one hundred. If I could get on to the roof of the skyscraper, I might have a chance of getting a signal from the Elite communications satellite. I jabbed my finger against the top button. As the lift climbed skywards, my mind raced ahead of it, already working out my next move.

Milo had said that the entire YourLife network was protected against cyber-attack. Even if I could patch Rez and Jimi back into the system, there was no guarantee they'd be able to shut the network down before Milo Bay launched it across the UK. I'd have to get Elliot to send in a team of commandos to close Milo Bay Industries down by force.

As I watched the floors go by, I saw a second number light up on the control panel, then a third and a fourth. Floors 47, 52, 63. More buttons pinged into life; their numbered lights filling the control panel. According to this, the lift was now going to call at every floor.

A rush of adrenalin kickstarted me into action, every nerve ending screaming with the realisation that I was heading into a trap. Milo Bay had every single person in this building hunting me down. I had to get out of here.

Bracing myself against the side of the lift, I reached up to open the hatch in its roof. I slid the metal panel backwards. The grinding noise of the lift gears was suddenly loud inside the cramped space. Hooking my fingers round the edge of the hatch, I hauled myself up, gritting my teeth as the sharp metal edges cut into my hands. I clambered up on top of the lift car just as it shuddered to a halt at the next floor.

With blood trailing from my fingers, I slipped the hatch cover back into position. Only a sliver of space remained. I pressed my face to the hatch and peered through this narrow gap as the lift doors below slid open.

Two security guards stepped into the lift. Each man had an assault rifle slung across his shoulder. Where on earth had they got those weapons from? Was Milo Bay building his own private army here?

I had to get in touch with Elite HQ before Elliot sent in a rescue team to try to pull me and Gems out of here. *It's the last option*, he'd told me before I'd left the base. *If you're not out of there before the YourLife network goes live, I'm sending a team to get you.* If they didn't know the firepower these guys were packing, there would be carnage.

Both men stood staring at their mobile phones as the lift doors closed. From my vantage point above their heads, I could see the YourLife interface shining out from both screens. Squinting, I could just make out a snatched photograph of my face and beneath this a one-word message:

Eliminate.

My heart thudded in my chest as I read the message. It felt so loud that I was almost surprised that the security guards couldn't hear it. If they just looked up …

The taller of the security guards reached for the lift's control panel. 'Which floor?' he asked. His voice sounded almost robotic.

His partner stared down at his phone as a message pinged on to its screen. 'Forty-four,' he replied in the same robotic tone.

I frowned. That was down and I needed to go up. Getting to the roof was my only chance of making contact with Elite HQ.

Lifting my head from the hatch, I stared up into the lift shaft for the first time. It was in complete darkness, except for a series of faint squares of light set back in the concrete walls. Ventilation ducts maybe. In the half light cast by the nearest of these, I saw a metal ladder reaching up into the darkness.

Then the lift cage juddered into life beneath my body. It began to descend, slowly at first, but then quickly picking up speed. Rising to a crouch, I reached out towards the wall. I had to time this just right.

I took a deep breath, flung myself forward and grabbed hold of the ladder. My trainers scrabbled for grip as the lift dropped away beneath me. Breathing hard, I clung to the ladder as the grinding of the lift gears finally squealed to a crescendo. The lift cage shudder to a stop two storeys below. Then, looking up into the darkness above, I began to climb.

CHAPTER EIGHTEEN

As I clambered up the ladder, the metallic clang of my steps echoed up the narrow shaft. My nerve endings jangled as I passed each floor. 50, 51, 52. Behind the closed lift doors, I could hear voices. The sound of Milo Bay's army of programmed assassins hunting their prey. Me. But here in the inky blackness of the lift shaft, I was safe.

Suddenly, I reached the end of the ladder. Glancing up, I could just make out a ten-metre stretch of empty wall before another ladder started again. I angrily banged the flat edge of my fist against the concrete. No way up.

Desperation filled my mind. Time was running out. If I didn't get a warning out before Milo Bay launched the YourLife network, then everyone in the country would be under his control.

Glancing around me, I glimpsed the thick twisted steel of the lift cables reaching up into the darkness. As I stared at the dangling cables, a crazy thought crept into my mind. If I could just climb up them for ten metres, then I could reach the ladder again.

I reached out with one hand for the nearest cable. I felt the woven steel beneath my fingers. Breathing hard, I tried to convince my body to trust my brain. I could do this. It would be just like climbing a rope in the school gym. I tried to forget how awful I was at PE.

Twisting my body, I leaned further across the lift shaft. Only my toes still kept a grip on the ladder. Under my breath, I kept on muttering the same three words: 'Don't look down.'

Grabbing hold of the lift cable with my other hand, I swung my body away from the ladder. Feeling the slippery steel start to slide through my fingers, I wrapped my legs round the cable. I tightened my grip and tried to ignore the blood running through my fingers. Then, sliding one hand above the other, I started to inch my way up.

From a ventilation duct a few metres above my head, a dull yellow light seeped into the lift shaft. As I climbed, I kept on glancing up at my target. The bottom rung of the ladder was getting nearer with every move I made. I was nearly a third of the way there now. Then, beneath me, I heard an ominous sound. The shrieking whirr of the lift gears grinding into life.

Beneath my fingers, the steel cable began to vibrate. I swore as my hold slipped, friction burning my fingers as the cable was hauled upwards. Below the lift car headed towards me. I felt a sudden rush of fear. It was going to wipe me out.

My hands scrabbled for a grip on the slippery steel cable. The lift cage below was speeding upwards. There was no way I could make it to the ladder in time. I didn't even know if I could hold on. Blood dripped though my fingers as the cable cut into my skin. My right hand slipped and, for a heart-wrenching moment, my legs kicked out against empty air.

I could hear the harsh grinding of gears more loudly now as the cage came towards me. If I fell now, it was all over.

With my hand flailing against the void, I reached up in desperation. My blood-slicked fingertips grabbed hold of the concrete sill just beneath the ventilation shaft. As the last reserves of strength ebbed from my body, I flung my other arm up, scrabbling for a handhold. Then, gritting my teeth against the pain, I hauled myself up as the lift shaft filled with a screeching howl.

I lay there exhausted, my face pressed against cold stone. Gasping for breath, I felt the concrete shake as the grinding gears of the lift cage passed centimetres from me. Inside, I heard the muffled sound of men's voices as the cage climbed above me. I let out a low moan of relief. I was alive.

Wincing, I pulled myself up into a crouching position and then glanced down at the bloodied mess of my hands. The steel cable had torn most of the skin from my palms. Fresh blood was oozing out and dripping between my fingers. I looked away in disgust, the pain making me sick to my stomach.

In front of me was a ventilation shaft. I could see a dim glow through the loose metal grate that covered the duct. Just big enough, maybe, for someone to crawl through. I glanced back up into the darkness and saw the lift cage come to a halt several floors above me. There was no way up now, but perhaps I could find a way around.

Ignoring the pain from my fingers, I wrenched back the grate and squeezed my way into the cramped shaft. As I crawled forward on my hands and knees, the sheet metal creaked beneath me. The ventilation shaft sloped upwards. Ahead of me, I could see another grate and, through this, the bright glare of strip lights. The muffled sound of footsteps and voices seeped through the grate. Beyond this, the shaft narrowed sharply, twisting upwards at an impossible angle. There was no way I could go any further.

Peeking through the grate, I tried to work out where I was. From my vantage point, I could see a long grey-carpeted corridor lit by fluorescent ceiling panels. Directly beneath these, I saw an armed band of office workers patrolling the corridor. Just like the security guards I had seen in the lift, they each held a mobile phone in one hand. In the other, they brandished broken chair legs, metal bars – anything they could use as a weapon.

I smiled grimly. This wasn't an office any more – it was a battlezone.

Waiting by the lift at the far end of the corridor was someone I had last seen on the screen of my laptop back at Elite HQ. The Milo Bay Industries employee in charge of training the new recruits: Blue-shirt Ben.

His phone was clamped to his ear and I strained my ears to listen in.

'I understand, sir,' he said, 'I'll head down to the bunker and run final checks on the system servers. YourLife goes live now.'

Hiding in the darkness of the ventilation shaft, despair filled my mind. Milo Bay was ready to brainwash the entire country. I was out of time.

CHAPTER NINETEEN

Peering through the grate, I watched powerlessly as Ben pressed the call button for the lift.

In my mind, I heard Milo Bay's transatlantic drawl. *I built the YourLife system myself*, he'd said. *Its computer servers are secured in a bunker beneath this skyscraper, which can withstand a direct nuclear strike.*

That was where Ben was going now. If I followed him, then maybe I could hack directly into the YourLife servers to take the network down. It was the only chance I had left.

But standing in my way were a dozen people who would kill me without a second thought. No chance of talking my way past them with the YourLife network in control of their minds. If only there was a way to switch off their programming.

That was it! During my training at Elite HQ, Gemma had showed me how to knock out any computer system at close range. All I needed was a mobile phone. I pulled my phone from my pocket, slid a bloodstained nail beneath its casing and prised the back off. Working quickly, I tried to remember exactly what Gems had showed me. Removing the battery compartment, I rewired the exposed circuit board. Pulling free a length of microscopic copper wire, I coiled this round the battery contacts and then clicked the compartment back into place. Done.

It wasn't a mobile phone any more – it was a bomb. All I needed to do now was press the call button and a low-level electromagnetic pulse would temporarily jam any electronics in a ten-metre radius. That was all I needed to take the YourLife zombies crowding this corridor offline. I just hoped the battery in my mobile would hold out long enough for me to reach the lift.

There was only one way to find out.

Kicking open the grate, I dropped down into the corridor, staggering a little as I landed. As a dozen dead-eyed stares swivelled towards me, I jabbed my finger against the call button. My mobile buzzed and then, all along the corridor, the office workers fell like dominoes to the floor. Their connection to the YourLife network had been switched off.

Only one person was left standing. As the lift doors pinged open, Ben was scrabbling for his own phone.

'Mr Bay,' he yelled. 'I've found him.'

As I raced down the corridor, Ben darted forward into the safety of the lift. I couldn't let him get away. Putting all my energy into a lung-bursting sprint, I slammed into the lift as the doors closed behind me. As he turned away from the control panel in surprise, I pressed my buzzing phone against his forehead.

'It's for you.'

Ben slumped to the floor unconscious, his brain overwhelmed by the electromagnetic pulse. I stepped over his body and studied the lift's control panel. The floors ran from Ground to 100, but there was no sign of any button to take me down to the bunker where the servers were stored. How was I supposed to get there?

My phone stopped buzzing as the battery finally died. I glanced down at Ben. In his hand, he was still holding his own mobile phone. I shook my head as a cautious smile crept across my face. Surely Milo Bay didn't use the same Bluetooth security key as the Elite. Lifting the phone from Ben's fingers, I pressed it against the control panel.

In reply, the panel buzzed and then the lift began to descend. My smile broke into a grin. Next stop – the bunker.

Leaning against the wall of the lift as it descended, I tried to work out what I would do when I got there. I should have been excited; adrenalin was already coursing through my veins. This was the chance I'd been waiting for: the opportunity to pit my cyber-skills against the world-famous Milo Bay, super-geek.

But this wasn't a game. The freedom of the whole world – billions of lives – was at stake. It could only have been a couple of minutes, but in my mind it felt like an age before the lift finally juddered to a halt. Then the doors slid open and I stepped out of the lift.

I was standing in a vast cavernous room, its high granite ceiling fused with steel. Banks of huge computer servers lined the walls, their silver casings blinking with thousands of green lights. All around, I could hear the roar of white noise – the cooling fans in the servers working to keep them at their optimum temperature.

This was the YourLife network. The brainwashing system Milo Bay had programmed was inside these computers. I had to shut it down before every single person in the UK logged on. The prime minister, the armed forces, even the Elite – they would all be under Milo Bay's control. In my mind, I could see Gemma walking towards me, her perfect face twisted into a murderous scowl.

I shook my head decisively. This stopped now.

In the centre of the room, a single computer was hooked up to the banks of servers. That was my way in.

Striding over to the computer, I glanced over its screen. Millions of names scrolled endlessly down the display as the YourLife system readied itself for launch.
I didn't have much time.

With quicksilver fingers, I tapped out a series of commands. The scrolling patterns of names froze before being replaced by a menu screen with the stark heading:

YourLife Control Centre

I was in.

My eyes flickered over the menu options:

Security and maintenance
Network updates
System settings
Connections
Additional options

All I needed to do was take the whole system offline. As I leaned forward over the computer, I felt a sudden rush of air whistling towards me. Then an explosion of pain detonated somewhere behind my eyes.

I staggered backwards, a rising red tide fogging my vision. Advancing towards me, his laidback smile now transformed into a snarl of hatred, was Milo Bay.

'You should have let me hook you up to the YourLife network,' he shouted over the deafening drone of the cooling fans. 'Life's so much easier if you just follow my orders. No need to think for yourself. Now I'm going to make you suffer.'

Without warning, he launched a devastating fusillade of bone-crunching blows, driving me backwards until I crashed against an emergency generator. Pain buzzed in my mind as I tried to pull myself to my feet.

Milo loomed above me, a cruel grin slashed across his face.

'Come on,' he sneered. 'Don't the Elite teach you how to fight?'

Reaching up as I scrabbled for a handhold, my fingers closed round a spanner left lying on the generator. I could feel the reassuring weight of it in my hand. It was time to fight back. As Milo drew his fist back ready to rain down another firestorm of blows, I slammed the spanner forward with all the strength I could muster, straight into his guts.

With a sharp grunt of pain, Milo sank to his knees. I heaved myself up from the generator.

'I'm the reigning *Fightstar* champion on the Xbox Kinect,' I told him, a thin line of blood trickling from my mouth. 'Beat that.'

'You little –' Milo hissed, still gasping for breath. 'I'm going to kill you.'

Rising like a rocket, he grabbed hold of my throat in a crushing vice-like grip. I staggered backwards, struggling to free myself, but Milo was too strong. As he squeezed the air from my lungs, I could feel the blood pounding in my brain. He was going to kill me.

I pushed my hand into Milo's face, trying in vain to break the death grip. In reply, he slammed me against the side of one of the huge servers, my head cracking against its metal casing. A red tide of unconsciousness overwhelmed me and I slid to the floor like a discarded rag doll.

Snarling with satisfaction, Milo strode to the central computer. He clicked on the Connections menu and then selected a single command.

'Welcome to my world,' he roared. 'The YourLife network is going live.'

Slumped half conscious against the cold white tiles, I was barely aware of Milo's roar of triumph. I stared up at the towering server through dulled eyes. Its cables and connections linked the YourLife network to the outside world. The white noise of the cooling fan filled my brain, the sound of it strangely soothing. It was too late to stop him now.

Next to the server's ventilation slots, I glimpsed a USB port – a back-up option to transfer data directly into the mainframe computer. A tiny chink in the indestructable armour Milo Bay had built around the YourLife network.

Suddenly, with a lurch of realisation, I knew how I could take the whole system down.

Fighting off the warm embrace of unconsciousness, I pulled myself up into a seated position. Quietly I scrabbled in the pocket of my overalls and drew out my USB key ring. Selecting the crimson-red memory stick, I inserted it into the server's empty USB port. The LED light on the side of the memory stick flashed red. Then the Apocalypse Worm started to burrow inside the YourLife servers.

I watched spellbound as a red tide swept across the banks of servers that filled the vast room. The Apocalypse Worm following its only command – to destroy. One by one, each server was infected, their lights blinking from green to red as the virus hungrily wiped the code of the entire YourLife network.

Standing in front of the central computer screen, Milo watched horrified as the YourLife interface froze and was replaced by a white screen of death.

'No!' he screamed. 'This can't be happening. YourLife is mine!'

He tried to reboot the system, but there was nothing there to save. The YourLife network was completely destroyed.

As the realisation hit home, Milo sank to the floor. Rising to my feet, I warily approached his crumpled form. Milo was holding his head in his hands, but through the gaps between his fingers, I saw his eyes were red with tears. The murderous youth was gone and in his place sat a miserable teenager.

I stared down at his defeated figure.

'It's over,' I told him.

CHAPTER TWENTY

Beneath the bunker's granite and steel dome, I sat in front of the central computer, slowly swivelling backwards and forwards on my chair. The bandages wrapped round my hands were already itching, but I tried to resist scratching them again. Next to me, Gemma sat with her head bent forward, holding a bloodstained tissue to her nose.

'Are you feeling OK now?' I asked her.

Twisting to face me, she nodded her head gingerly.

'Yeah, I think my nose has finally stopped bleeding.' The edges of her mouth creased in a smile. 'I've just got this splitting headache from Milo Bay screaming his orders into my brain.'

I smiled back at her. Neither of us could hide our relief that we'd got out of this mission alive.

All around me, a team of white-suited technicians were carefully dismantling the computer servers that lined the walls. They were packing them up to take away to a secret Elite research station. There, they would painstakingly reassemble the system to see if any trace of Milo Bay's YourLife programming lurked on the hard drives.

I turned towards Elliot who was standing a few metres away, watching the technicians with a furrowed brow.

'So what happens now?'

Elliot glanced back towards us.

'Milo Bay Industries has been taken over,' he said. 'The US government has bought all of Milo Bay's shares at a knockdown price. We're just doing a little asset-stripping here before the new owners arrive.'

'What about Milo Bay?' Gemma asked.

'He's checked into an exclusive Swiss clinic,' Elliot replied. 'We're putting out the report that he's suffering from nervous exhaustion. It's always the way with these teenage geniuses. They shine brightly at first, but they always burn out.'

Seeing the shock on my face, the corners of Elliot's mouth turned up in a thin-lipped smile.

'Don't worry. His stay in the clinic is scheduled to be a long one. MI6 will keep Milo Bay under constant surveillance for the rest of his life. He'll never be let near a computer again. The most technologically advanced piece of kit he'll ever own will be a digital watch.'

Gemma grinned.

'You did well, Luke,' Elliot continued. 'Although it was a shame you had to use the Apocalypse Worm to wipe out the YourLife network. The YourLife programming could have proved useful to us here at the Elite.'

I frowned at the thought. Nobody should have the power to control another person's mind. Not even the Elite.

'Sorry about that,' I replied. 'It was either that or let Milo Bay take over the world.'

'Don't worry,' said Elliot, ignoring the sarcasm in my voice. 'I'm sure you'll do better next time. After all, you're a fully fledged Elite agent now.'

Glancing at Gemma, we shared a secret grin. This was my life now. Luke Kitson – Elite agent. I couldn't wait for my next mission.

THE END

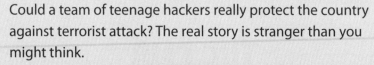

Could you be a cyber-spy?

The truth behind the world of i-SSASSINS

Could a team of teenage hackers really protect the country against terrorist attack? The real story is stranger than you might think.

In 2010, the British government named cyber terrorism as one of the main threats facing the country. Experts believe that cyber terrorists could use computers to:

- hack into government websites to steal secrets;
- take control of military equipment, such as spy satellites;
- shut down the power grid, leaving the country without electricity;
- take over air traffic control systems, causing planes to crash out of the sky.

Anything that is controlled by a computer is at risk in a cyber-attack. This could be a life-support machine in a hospital or the reactor at a nuclear power plant. In today's digital world, the entire country could grind to a halt because of a cyber attack.

Teenage spies

To help protect the country from this threat, the security services at MI5 and MI6 decided to recruit some new blood. They set up a cyber-security team run by computer hackers.

Lord West, a security expert, said the government needed naughty boys who knew computers to help catch the hackers.

The job of this team of top-secret agent geeks is to:

- identify any cyber-attacks launched against the UK;
- find out where the attacks are coming from;
- stop the attacks.

The team are based at the Cyber-Security Centre at GCHQ (Government Communications Headquarters) in the west of England. Tom Watson, a former junior defence minister in the British government, said GCHQ needs to become a spy school for computer geeks.

Geeks international

The UK isn't the only country that recruits young computer hackers. The United States of America runs a nationwide competition called the Cyber Challenge. This competition aims to find 10,000 young people with the computer skills needed to become top cyber-spies.

Cyber-warfare

Some countries have already come under cyber-attack. In 2007, the US Army, Air Force and Navy's computer network was hacked into by cyber terrorists. This cyber-attack was given the code-name 'Titan Rain'. The cyber terrorists shut down the email system of the man in charge of US defence. Some reports say that the cyber terrorists also stole top-secret information.

Nobody knows for sure who was behind the 'Titan Rain' attacks. However, experts believe that the cyber terrorists could have been working for a foreign government trying to steal American secrets.

Hacking attacks have also brought whole countries to a standstill. The country of Estonia found itself under cyber-attack in 2007. Using ping attacks and botnets, hackers shut down the websites of Estonia's TV stations, newspapers, banks and even the government itself.

These cyber-attacks came from computers around the world. In total, nearly one million computers were used. To stop their websites from being swamped, Estonia had to cut off its Internet connections to the rest of the world. The hackers had shut the country down.

Ping attack

A ping attack is a special type of cyber-attack. It works by flooding a computer or Web server with repeated requests for information, sent hundreds of times every second. This causes the computer to crash.

Botnet

A botnet is a network of computers that have been taken over by hackers. These computers are called zombies, and hackers use them to flood websites with useless data. This clogs up the website and takes it offline.

Could you make it as a cyber-spy?

What skills do you need as a cyber-spy? Obviously it helps if you're a hotshot computer expert. You need to know that a computer virus isn't a cold that you catch from a laptop and that worms can live online and not underground!

However, to make it as a spy you need to be more than just a techno-wiz. A good spy needs to be able to:

- **handle dangerous situations:** Whether breaking into a top-secret research lab or following an enemy agent, you don't know what might be lurking around the corner. Have you got the quick wits you need to take care of yourself?

- **keep calm under pressure:** When working undercover you need to keep your identity secret. If someone suspects you're a spy, they could blow your cover. Could you keep a cool head when being grilled by the enemy?

- **learn quickly:** As a spy, you might need to go anywhere in the world. Could you learn a new language and the skills needed for your undercover identity?

Worms and viruses

- A virus is a program that infects the files on your computer. They can spread from computer to computer if the infected files are shared. A virus can wipe the contents of your computer's hard drive.

- A worm is a type of virus that spreads itself. Worms do this by using the contacts in your e-mail address book. The worm e-mails copies of itself to every contact and infects their computers too.

Spy-tech

In the movies, spies are always kitted out with hi-tech gadgets. However, you might find all the kit you need to be a spy on your mobile phone.

- **Tracking device**: Many mobile phones now have GPS (Global Positioning System) fitted. If you are trying to follow an enemy agent, you could slip your phone into their pocket and the GPS system will tell you where they go.

- **Spy camera**: The camera on your mobile could be useful if you need to copy top-secret papers in a hurry.

- **Listening device**: If your mobile has a voice recorder, this will let you record and listen back to anyone you are spying on.

- **Spy apps**: There are many apps that would be useful to a spy on a mission. If you're on a mission in a foreign country, you could use an app that translates other languages into English. Think that someone might have a hidden weapon? There's even an app that turns your phone into a metal detector.

When you log on to your computer or send a message from your mobile phone, think about who could be watching you. Remember the cyber-spies are out there!

We would like to thank the following schools and students for all their help in developing and trialling *i-SSASSINS*.

Darland High School, Wrexham

Emma Scott, Craig Baines, Lydia Evans, Hannah Lucas, Nia Radley, Alix Godfrey, Nathan Taylor, Alice Eccles, Leanna Baugh, Aidan Nicklin, William Roberts, George Tucker, Dominic Leeder, Darren Povey, Zara Louise Owens.

Risley Primary School, Haringey

Akeim Akenzua, Hibaaq Ashkir, Tyreece Paul-Coleman, Selen Demirkaya, Alwx Dong, Lava Fariq, Esel Fedail, Kimonie Hanchard, Mohamed Hassan, Arifa Khanom, Askim Kisacik, Scarlett Kolomiychenko, Michella Lambert, John McDonagh, Melissa Michaelides, Ali Mohammed, Ayesha Moothien, Alfie Morley, Wesley Ngombe, Longwani Nkwabilo, Siobhan Osman, Cagla Parker, Leyanne Quarry, Ja'vay Thompson, Shaelle Twum-Barimah, Constantion Zachariou, Pavlina Zachariou.

To find out more about Christopher Edge and his books,
visit www.christopheredge.co.uk